Real Ghost Stories of Borneo Book 4

Real First Accounts of Ghost Encounters

By
Dr. Aammton Alias

Copyright ©2020 Aammton Alias, M Content Creations
All Rights Reserved

Cover design by Ariz & Bob

ISBN: 978-1-71668-870-6

Please visit my website at http://www.b1percent.com

Permission to reproduce or transmit in any form or by any means, electronic or mechanical, including photocopying and recording, or by an information storage and retrieval system, must be obtained by writing to the author via email:

author@b1percent.com

For enquiries on obtaining printed books, please email:
now@b1percent.com

Dedicated

to

'Deen'

Muhammad Burhanudeen Jaleel

You were a sincere and patient friend,
a beloved son,
a loving husband,
a compassionate father,
a caring brother …
you will be missed.

Deen or Burhan was well known as
he was our frontman for
marketing and product info.
We were together as buddies and
business partners for almost 25 years.
Together we created niche concerts,
expo, fashion show and souvenir gifts supplier.
He will be remembered deeply in our hearts
Bless our Brother.

- Mike and the Alhamdulillah group

CONTENTS PAGE

Acknowledgments 7
Introduction: Quattro 9
The Study Companion 11
The Serdang Incident 19
The Other House at Kebangsaan Road 28
The Passenger 35
The Banyan Tree 40
A Raya Story 53
The Residents 64
The New Job Challenges 72
Camping at the Beach 81
The Photo 94
The Fern Misadventure 111
The New Hostel 120
The Jungle Mission 128
The Noisy Neighbour 138
The Dormitory: 1992 145
The Uneasy Student 151

The Clinic on the Hill: Part 1	157
The Clinic on the Hill: Part 2	162
The Dare	167
Toyols	175
Part 1	175
Part 2	179
The Cicada	182
About The Author	189
What Happens After This?	190
Upcoming Books for 2020	191
My Other Books	194

Real Ghost Stories of Borneo 4

Acknowledgments

I never thanked him enough. The late Deen not only gave the idea for me to write this book series but tolerated my initial skepticism and near ridicule comments.

He kept nagging me to undertake this project: Real Ghost Stories of Borneo series. Without his persistence and his good intentions, this book series would not have materialized.

His passing away is not just a loss to our reading and literacy community but it is a stark reminder to be thankful for our dear friends and family who have helped us along the way and enriched our lives with moments and wise words. The importance of showing our gratitude and appreciation for others whilst they are still around, is only blindingly obvious once their time is gone.

I thank my daughter, Erica, who had helped in my writing, and had also had a stint at writing up one of the stories for me. She is an eagle-eyed proofreader and has been supportive of her father's endeavours.

I thank my tireless wife, Azfa, who continues to support me in my writing life mission. She is part of my proofreading and story development team. Whilst I am sleeping, she goes through what I have written and gives me feedback after my naps. My wife is also the person who ensures I wake up on time to write my next story.

My good friend Dr. Jawad Khan, who is both a family physician and an author, had provided me with unconditional support and editorial advice since the beginning, since the first book I had ever written. He has been pivotal in my writing career development. I cannot thank him enough. I usually write stories within stories about him in all of my books, as a way to celebrate our friendship.

I heartfully thank the story contributors for this fourth book. I also thank the many contributors who chose to remain anonymous.

This book was made possible thanks to a successful PRE-ORDER campaign from loyal readers. Most of my loyal readers have also supported my previous pre-order campaigns for the other books in the series and beyond.

Last but not least, I thank the support of my compatriots in the Reading & Literacy Association (RELA). Together we will instill the reading and writing culture amongst our people.

Introduction: Quattro

I was supposed to write two books during the coronavirus disease or covid-19 'movement restriction order' in my country. Personally, I would classify it as a partial lockdown. I was still working in the private clinic but saw very few patients. I realised that I needed to see and talk to people to hear their stories in order to write. Having ample time was not enough.

During this post-covid pandemic world, we wake up to a new perspective and take into account what we had taken for granted. The world has changed far more than before, and we must heed the signs.

As I wrote this book, I tried to figure out what the damn theme is this time. The truth is I failed so hard, laughing at myself was the only relief. Initially, when close friends asked, I surmised the phrase: 'rojak', which generally means a mix-up.

However, as I am about to go to print, I realised that this book is about time and memory. It goes back to a personal core value, which is of making **connection** and **time**. As we move through life and become wiser, we should realise it is never about the networks we create, but about the deep relationships with the very few that we nurture and cherish through the limitations of time.

I hope you take this with you as you read through my book. It is not simply about the horrors of ghost and supernatural encounters. There is much more if you choose to delve deeper in between the lines.

In any case, I hope you have a good fright and stay safe, maintaining social distancing, for whatever reasons it may be.

The Study Companion

A university student friend had heard a few versions of this 'recent' spiritual encounter.

Ahmad was a Mathematics fresher undergrad at the University. When he noticed that his mid-semester grades were appalling, he decided to spend more time concentrating on his studies instead of hanging out with his friends who loved to surf at Tungku beach. He could not afford to fail and be kicked out of university, especially in the first year.

It was not a matter of honor, pride or ego. He had a need. His father had recently been unwell. Being unable to work in the piping industry, he was quickly made redundant with no form of compensation. His mother worked as a janitor at a nearby school, whilst his eldest sister, who could not get a job, was earning a meagre amount from selling 'nasi katok' or chicken and chilli rice dish at a roadside makeshift stall. Ahmad was the hope for the family to uplift them from their destitution.

Being with his well-off friends, he would usually forget his home issues and would stay at the beach from late afternoon till evening. After riding out the not-so-tall waves on their surfboards, they would watch the sunset whilst discussing life and everything but Ahmad's family. Ahmad was good at changing the topic every time someone broached his family. When the sun had set and it became dark, they would head home. With each passing day, Ahmad dreaded heading home. He hated being poor. He wished his parents had done better for themselves, instead of depending on their eldest son to lift them up from hopelessness.

Ahmad did not want to be at home. He decided he should hit the books at the University Library. The University Library was a multi-storey library. Usually, it closed at 9pm, though sometimes it closed much later. Ahmad went up to the third floor, as he did not want to be bothered. He knew most students would be at the ground and first floors. No one would usually go to the third floor, which meant it would be silent and he could concentrate.

When he got to the third floor, there was not a soul present other than his. It was so quiet that he could hear a soft ringing sound in his ears. Library bookshelves lined and surrounded the rows of wooden tables. Ahmad chose to sit at the table at the end which would give him the perfect view of the floor. If there were any students, he figured they were unlikely to walk all the way to his table.

As he did his coursework, he could smell the scent of the sea. He was sure the scent was coming from his hands. Extra fine sea salt must have crystallised on his hands and resisted washing away. He sniffed his hands and took a deep breath in. As he began to miss the sea, he experienced a body memory; a visceral floating in the open sea. Ahmad snapped himself out of those thoughts and convinced himself that he had to bite the bullet and do well in his exams.

He took out his mobile phone, doing his best to avoid looking at his Instagram and TikTok accounts, selected an internet music playlist which he listened through his earphones. The streaming online upbeat music would drown the deafening silence and help him concentrate on his Maths studies.

Ahmad quickly gained momentum in his studies, furiously highlighting notes and rechecking mathematical formulae relevant to his coursework. He had forgotten the call of the sea, his woes and his hopes and dreams, choosing to be lost in mathematics' enigma.

Even when the air in the vast room had gotten colder, Ahmad was able to shake it off and continue in complete concentration. However, he was interrupted when his phone stopped streaming music to his ears. He could not connect to the library Wi-Fi as it kept disconnecting him.

He glanced at his phone and saw his mobile phone no

longer had a signal reception, whether it was 4G or 3G. He cursed the telcos for charging exorbitantly and yet providing poor mobile phone service, which was a common complaint amongst his countrymen.

"Yeah, I know sometimes there's no mobile phone reception here," A male voice spoke to him.

It jolted Ahmad. He had not noticed anyone climb up to the floor, let alone walk all the way to his table. He looked up and saw a youthful man of around his age, with clothes similar to his standing next to his table.

He continued, "But it does make this floor the perfect quiet spot, no?"

Ahmad nodded, and before Ahmad could say anything else, the visitor introduced himself, "I am Saifuddin. May I sit next to you? Because I don't want to be all alone on this floor."

Ahmad reached out to shake hands with Saifuddin, but Saifuddin did not wait for Ahmad's approval, or handshake; he quickly sat next to Ahmad.

Ahmad understood that Saifuddin too needed to study or he must have a deadline.

He knew this was not the time to make idle chatter. This was a library after all, and they both had to concentrate on their work. Ahmad tried his best to pick up his studying momentum, but he was not used to quiet studying. He really needed the music in his ears. The soft ringing sensation only seemed to grow louder and louder.

Ahmad tapped on the wooden table with his pen. Saifuddin did a subtle cough, which Ahmad picked up as a hint not to carry on with that habit. There was another thing that was bothering Ahmad, and it was becoming far more annoying than the ringing sound.

It was the foul smell that was becoming more noticeable with every passing moment. It was as though someone had left a garbage can open. He wondered if it was Saifuddin. He leaned slightly towards him and took a gentle whiff, but the smell did not seem to originate from him. It seemed to come from all directions.

Unintentionally, Ahmad began to tap again with his pen, and Saifuddin responded again with a subtle cough. This time, it startled Ahmad, and he lost grip of his pen and the pen rolled off the table and onto the floor.

"Sorry," Ahmad muttered softly.

He stooped down to pick up the pen, and as he was about to get himself back up, Ahmad became petrified at a shocking discovery: Saifuddin's body ended at his mid-torso, he had no legs or buttocks!

Ahmad hit his head to the table and knew he was in big trouble. Doing his best not to look at Saifuddin, he picked up his books and excused himself.

"I suddenly feel very tired, I better go home now."

He carefully walked away, his body rigid in betrayal to his attempt to remain composed. Ahmad's eyes were focused on the exit.

"Wah, you have to go home so soon. I thought we could be friends," Saifuddin's voice seemed deeper and huskier than before.

Ahmad felt shiveringly cold and the hairs on his arms were raised in alarm. He had to keep walking and whatever might happen, Ahmad did not want to turn around to look at Saifuddin.

Ahmad could hear Saifuddin's heavy breathing echoing in the library, "Are you really that tired?"

Ahmad chose not to respond and kept walking away. He was now half-way across to the exit. He clutched his books ever more tightly.

"Or... coz' you already know?" Saifuddin's voice came from next to Ahmad's right ear, it was growl-like and demonic!

Real Ghost Stories of Borneo 4

Ahmad took no chances. He sprinted to the end of the room, praying the exit doors, which were always open, would not suddenly close on him. There was a deafening roar from behind him. Ahmad had cleared the doorway, but he could hear his pursuer was not stopping there.

The doorway led to a few flights of stairs. With enough momentum, Ahmad did the one thing he knew that he could do. He jumped and flew across an entire flight of stairs, landing on his feet on to a lower landing.

With little thought, he picked himself up and jumped across another flight of stairs. This time, however, Ahmad fell short of the landing on the second floor, and instead, he tripped on the stairs and twisted his ankle and foot to an unnatural position. His body rolled in an unceremonious manner. He landed hard on the second floor, tumbling before coming to an abrupt stop.

His body was aching everywhere, and his foot was in tremendous pain. Ahmad tried to clamber, but the pain was too excruciating that he began screaming loudly, which did nothing to subside his pain. A black figure approached him slowly from the staircase. He knew without a doubt that this was 'Saifuddin'. He crawled away from him but he could barely move as he was paralysed with both fear and pain.

"Are you okay? What happened?" A woman's voice shattered the chilling situation.

Saifuddin had disappeared, and Ahmad became aware he was being attended to by one of the librarians, who was quickly accompanied by two other librarians and a crowd of student onlookers.

One librarian had muttered under her breath, "I hate these students when they run in the library, what a drama!"

They had to call the ambulance as Ahmad was in significant pain, and he was looking very bewildered.

It turned out that he had broken his left ankle and had to be on crutches. His friends visited him at home for the next few days. At first, Ahmad felt shameful of his family, but his friends assured him they cared little about his family or social background. A few of his other friends even confided that they were proud of what he was doing for his family.

Whilst he was still on crutches, every time Ahmad went to study in the library, his friends would tag along with him. They would all be on the ground floor.

Real Ghost Stories of Borneo 4

The Serdang Incident

During my college years, I had an old friend named Salim, who used to share with me several of his ghost encounters. Back then, I did not believe him. I simply obliged in his tales and thought he was merely superstitious and had jumped to my mis-led own conclusions. That was probably why he never shared the full account of his encounters. Having read my books, we met up, and he shared one of his supernatural encounters.

In the year 1999, Salim was a 28-year-old postgraduate student studying abroad in the United Kingdom. He would return home during the Summer holidays to spend time with his family. He lived in Serdang Village, which is in in Kota Batu, the so-called 'Brunei Riviera'. Their house was on the hilly side of Kota Batu, which faced the river, and they had a splendid view from there. The national museum also known as Kota Batu Museum is situated nearby.

During this time, Salim, along with his father and his two brothers, would hike around the Subok Hills. The ridges around this area faced the water village or 'Kampong Ayer'. It was a time to bond between the four men of the family. They would watch the sunset from the hilltops.

On one occasion, the four of them would do a night walk along the same ridges. They knew the area very well, like the back of their hands, and were confident of their abilities during this night walk. Their idea was to gaze upon the starry night sky from the hilltops. One of Salim's brothers objected, but their father thought they should go ahead, as this was a 'bucket-list' for everyone.

After evening prayers, they packed up water and emergency rations, and brought their torchlights and their best and sole safety equipment, i.e. a parang or machete. The emergency ration was hardly needed, but it was a matter of preparing for the unexpected. As the local saying goes, it is best to 'bring along the umbrella, in case it rains."

Salim's father and his sons set off into the dark starry night and headed towards their favourite hilltop spot. To get there, they had to negotiate a dirt pathway through the jungle.

As they got deeper into the jungle, the jungle got noisier and noisier with the hoots, buzzing, shrieks, calls, caws and snorts of the jungle's night creatures and critters.

Salim's father led the way through the dark. He did not use his torchlight. He could see in the dark, and he knew the terrain well enough that he could walk there blindfolded if he needed to.

Real Ghost Stories of Borneo 4

Salim had his fears. He was terrified of what could go wrong on such a nightly expedition, as his mind was always being prepared for the worst-case scenario. Some would say it was paranoia, but it turned out to help in his future career.

Anyway, every time Salim's father sensed doubt in Salim or his brothers, Salim's father would stop and utter motivational keywords, such as trust, dauntless, instinct, courage, brotherhood and family. In the past, Salim's father had told motivational stories, and he had cued those keywords to trigger a recall of those stories when his sons had doubt or felt insecure.

In a short time, the four of them reached their hill spot and were immediately awed by the majestic moonless night sky filled with billions of stars, some twinkling brighter than others. To them, it was an ordained canvas painted for their eyes only. In that timeless moment, they were grateful to be alive, to be healthy and to be with each other.

Salim's father eventually signaled for everyone to head home. As they thread through the jungle, they sensed the jungle trees had changed somehow. The trees looked the same in the darkness, but something immaterial had occurred. Salim thought he saw, in the corner of his eye, a slender ominous figure standing on a large branch of one tree, and as they picked up their pace, he saw that the figure was hopping from tree to tree. Salim did his best not to look at it directly. They arrived home with no incident.

The next evening, Salim's father and his brothers insisted they go to the same spot to watch the stars. Nothing had happened when they were heading to the much-adored stargazing spot. It was the trip back that caused alarm.

This time it was not just Salim who would see the shadowy figure standing on top of the biggest branches of the biggest tree in the jungle. They did their best to ignore, but Salim felt compelled to confirm what his eyes were seeing and turned his head to stare at it.

Immediately, Salim was struck on his face and chest. Initially, he did not know how he was hit, and that alarmed him. Then, much to his relief, he realised he had run into his brother!

Salim's father noticed the commotion and stopped. Salim was about to explain what he saw, but his father gestured for him to ignore it and to stay quiet. He instructed his sons to go ahead and he would be behind them. In the corner of their eyes they could see 'it' was following them. They picked up their pace, but their pursuer did not stop chasing after them, jumping effortlessly from tree to tree. The four of them were nearly running through the jungle pathway. It was only when they got to the car park that they saw no sign of whatever was after them.

The Serdang Incident by @krkdile

The next evening, no one suggested that they partake in stargazing on the hilltops. Little did they realise that 'it' had already followed them to their house in Serdang village.

In the middle of the night, when everyone else was fast asleep, it began with a tapping on the window of Salim's bedroom. His bedroom was on the ground-floor. The tapping was eccentric. There was a single knocking or double knocking, but never three times in a row. Salim did not believe it was a bird or even an insect.

Although the outside of his bedroom window was dark and a thin set of curtains covered the window, he could make out an outline of a tall shadow figure in the darkness. Salim figured that as long as he ignored it and he did not open the window; he would be safe. Salim believed prayers and love protected the house.

The next evening after that, the same thing had occurred. A part of him wanted to open the window and shout at the potential intruder. This was his house, after all. But he did not. He restrained himself from acting on his inner impulses.

The same thing had happened on the third night. Finally, on the fourth night, Salim called his two younger brothers and asked them to wait with him until after midnight. With the lights switched off, the 3 of them stayed in bed and listened intently. Sure enough, there was the same consistent single and double tapping sequence on his bedroom window. Through the thin window curtains, the other two brothers could see an outline of the tall shadow-like figure!

In the morning, the three of them decided it was best to confront the entity that was knocking on Salim's window. They drew up plans, as suggested by his younger brother. The plan was to have Salim and his youngest brother stand a distance away from the window and then his middle brother would draw open the curtains whilst keeping his eyes closed and his head facing down towards the floor. His middle brother was supposed to be the bravest! He would be nearest to the window and if anything were to happen, Salim and his youngest brother were to pull him away from the window if necessary! They all agreed on the plan.

They had prepared everything, including flashlights and bottles of 'blessed' water in case of an 'abduction'. They brought mattresses from the other bedrooms to Salim's bedroom so they could stay on guard comfortably. Although all three brothers were in their 20s, it felt like a teenage school weekend night adventure.

As they were getting ready, a loud knocking suddenly interrupted the three of them. It was not coming from the window. It was coming from inside the house. A voice emanated from inside the house. It was Salim's father!

Salim's father was curious about what his boys were up to and when they explained everything, the boys had expected their father to tell them to 'carry on' which was a common thing for army officers to say to their soldiers. To their surprise, their father told them not to do any such thing, but they may sleep together in the room for that night.

Left to their devices, Salim and his brothers prepared for their confrontation.

In anticipation, they watched the clock tick away the silent night. However, nothing happened. There was no knocking on the window by any supernatural entity, and they all slept soundly that evening.

Strangely enough, it was the only evening that there was no window knocking incident. After that, it continued on every night in Salim's room.

Deciding not to confront it, Salim bought a small radio and placed it near the windowsill. In the evenings he would switch to the Quran radio channel. He made sure the volume was loud enough to drown out any window tapping. This became a ritual for Salim throughout his 'summer vacation'. There was no further tapping in the middle of the night.

The next year, whilst Salim was away in the United

Real Ghost Stories of Borneo 4

Kingdom, Salim's father had built a new house in a suburb and rented his old house to a construction company. The company needed housing for their Indonesian workers. One particular Indonesian construction worker was back early from his holiday and slept alone in Salim's former bedroom.

That evening, an unseen entity awoke him violently and the worker found himself pinned down onto his bed. He could hardly breathe. Someone or something was sitting on his chest. He could see a blurred shadow outline of a human-like figure. He recited Holy Verses and only then did the intruder disappear into thin air and he could free himself. Salim's father told him of Salim's practice and hence even to this day the radio is switched on to the Quran channel and left on for 24-hours a day.

Salim was grateful that he had never had such frightening experiences.

Dr Aammton Alias

The Other House at Kebangsaan Road

My good friend Deen had recently passed away on the 11th July 2020. I recall when I was talking to him about writing the next ghost book, he shared a personal ghost story. However, at that time, I had already written two other stories about supernatural encounters at Kebangsaan Road.

It seems every 'Real Ghost Stories of Borneo' book has a ghost story related to this area. There are also several other Kebangsaan Road stories, which I have not yet published, so it is making me wonder what is happening there.

Deen and his family had rented a house at a cul-de-sac in Kebangsaan Road area. They considered it a good deal as the house had a below-market rental, which was a 'steal' as the area was strategic.

It was near the National Stadium Sports complex and the Capital where his office store was located. Deen's mother, his sister, and his brother were living with them. It was an exciting time when moving to a sizable house. Everyone in his family rushed to stake claim to the rooms of their choice, which was later re-suited to those in priority i.e. eldest got to choose first.

Real Ghost Stories of Borneo 4

One of their neighbours was an elderly Chinese couple, who had a Filipino maid. They had never met the elderly couple, but they had gotten acquainted with the Filipino maid, Mary. In the beginning, she seemed reserved in getting to know her new neighbours.

A few weeks later, when Deen's family thought they had settled down, they started noticing irregularities. Sometimes, Deen and his family members noticed some rooms would get cold suddenly, even though the fan had been switched off. At other times, they would notice an ominous sensation that they were not alone in the empty room.

Soon after that, Deen discovered some furniture and items had been moved during the night. Another time, things like keys and rings would go missing for a few days, and no matter how hard they searched, they could not find them. When they gave up, the missing items would reappear in the same spot they had usually left them.

Eventually, Deen got tired and called up his Bangladeshi friend who was an 'Imam' of some kind. The 'Imam' guy named Yusuf came to his house and did a spiritual cleansing in the house. He said there were powerful spirits that were living in the house and they had scared the previous tenants away.

Yusuf pointed to the hill behind their house, "They come from there, and own this entire valley at Kebangsaan Road."

Deen was puzzled and became more concerned to which Yusuf assured him he had evicted the spirits and they won't bother his house.

The next day around dusk time, Deen's brother, Harun, was out in the backyard, fixing his bicycle when something in the background had stirred his every emotion. A large shadowy figure was running down the hill. The entity was as tall as a two-storey building, and it was rushing towards him. Although it was faceless, he could sense it was angry and had every intent to hurt.

Harun wanted to run away, run to the safety of his house, but he was frozen in terror. His breathing had gotten shallower, and he found himself even more breathless. He had never seen one before, but he knew this was an 'Orang Tinggi' demon. It got closer and closer to him with every passing second.

Harun wanted so much to scream, but nothing came out of his mouth. The Orang Tinggi was immediately before the fence of his backyard. Harun had no chance to escape. From the fence, the Orang Tinggi demon's long arms could snatch and kill him.

Miraculously, when the demon attempted to cross, it

rebounded and then the entity slid forcibly along the fence and went straight into his neighbour's house. It disappeared without a trace.

Fazed by the unexplained, Harun dropped his bicycle and sprinted into the house. He stumbled and picked himself up, not stopping as he dashed into his room and jumped into his bed, with his shoes still on.

He remained in his bed, under his blanket. He had no other safe place he could think of, as sweat poured out non-stop from his shivering body to a point the bed was soaked with the sweat of fear.

He wished he had covered his windows with permanent covers, like aluminum foil. This was not an uncommon practice in the blazing tropical country. Although he had shut his eyes tight and kept himself hidden under the thin blanket, he felt demonic prying eyes with vengeful desires, staring through the windows onto him.

Harun kept praying for his safety, reciting as many Holy verses as he could until he fell asleep from the exhaustion of fearing.

When he woke up the next day, he confided with Deen on what had transpired.

"I guess Imam Yusuf protected our house," Deen laughed, half believing his brother. They went to work without a single doubtful thought. When they came back home for lunch, the brothers felt a dreary change in the atmosphere.

There was a recognisable purple fabric hanging inside their neighbour's house. Several cars were parked outside and in the driveway. There was no doubt that there had been a death in that house.

Since they were not well acquainted with their neighbour, Deen and his brother opted not to visit the house. It was best to let them grief in private; though, they waited for an opportunity to meet Mary, the Filipino maid.

Eventually, Mary came out to hang and dry the laundry in the backyard. When she had finished, the brothers called out to Mary, and enquired on what had happened.

Mary revealed that yesterday evening, the elderly Chinese lady in the house had suddenly passed away. Mary was sobbing and trembling as she tried to utter the words, "They told us it was a heart attack or just old age, but she was very healthy."

The brothers nodded as they tried to console her, but Mary had more to say, "Last night, it attacked her, I saw it with my own eyes! A giant demon. It had no face, and it was all black. Somehow it came into the house! I don't know if we are safe tonight!" Mary was hysterical as she tried to calm herself down with each sob.

Before Mary could say anything else, a younger family member of the deceased called her in.

The revelation shocked the two brothers, as they pieced together what they believed to be the correct version of the event. They wondered if protecting their house had left the other houses in their neighbourhood to be vulnerable.

Deen called up Imam Yusuf, who reassured him the death was probably unrelated. He went on to say that angry spirits usually go after the people who took away their 'property'.

Imam Yusuf laughed and promised he would visit them the next day. Imam Yusuf would inspect their house and the surrounding area and protect the whole neighbourhood if he could.

The next day after work, Deen and his brother waited for Imam Yusuf, but he did not turn up. Deen tried calling, but his call was unanswered.

"Maybe he meant tomorrow, instead of today," Harun suggested. They waited at the same time the next day. But as far as Deen was concerned, Imam Yusuf did not fulfill his promise. The very thought of breaking a promise annoyed Deen.

It was only a few days later that they found out that Imam Yusuf had mysteriously died on the evening of their fated phone call. Deen was scared that further harm would come to his family. He sought advice from his friend and mentor, Bob, who advised him not to move.

To his relief, Deen and his family did not experience any other supernatural encounters. Their neighbours i.e. the widower and Mary eventually moved away. A young Chinese family moved in and did not seem to have any issues with their stay.

Nevertheless, Deen tried his best to move from the house, but due to pricing and housing shortages, they ended up staying at the house for the next few years later.

Real Ghost Stories of Borneo 4

The Passenger

I am a busy working mother, balancing between the rigors of a demanding career and the needs of my husband and my three daughters. My daughters Wafa, Syasya and Syifa are aged 8, 5 and 1 years old.

Sundays are special to us, as it was our family day. One Sunday, my husband had a work commitment, so I had taken my three daughters and our Indonesian maid, Warsini, to visit my mother. My mother lived in Tanjong Maya village, which was in a different district, i.e. Tutong district.

We had spent the entire day at my mother's house, and when it was after dusk or after Maghrib prayer, we headed home. I was not keen to drive late at night from Tutong, especially through the 'white sands' area of Tutong.

For those who are unaware, white silica sand can be seen on both sides of the Tutong highway and the surrounding areas. The sand is so white, especially when seen from afar, that it looks like snow! Occasionally, you get the odd fellow and gal who would dress up in winter clothing and take snapshots in the tropical white sands of Tutong. As per local urban myths, there have been many supernatural sightings and experiences at the Tutong white sands area, which have made me reluctant to drive through the area at night, especially without my husband.

When we left my mother's house, my eldest daughter Wafa had the privilege of being my wingman i.e. she sat in the front passenger seat. Of course, that privilege came with responsibilities such as setting up the DVD system with my daughters' favourite movies. I drive a large four-wheel-drive SUV and it was equipped with three LCD display screens; one in front and two at the back. I know people may say this is not healthy living for children, but it keeps my children comfortable, especially on long trips from the Capital to Tutong. More importantly, it keeps them from distracting me whilst I drive, hence it has been a safety issue for me.

However, trouble struck even before we had reached the Tutong highway. I had driven out onto the main Tanjong Maya road, when out of the blue, my youngest daughter, Syifa, who was sitting on my maid's lap began screaming and crying. As though, in synchrony, the car engine had stalled and died. I panicked, as there was a car heading towards us. I tried to restart the car, and it did not respond. I uttered a quick prayer and turned the ignition key, and luckily, the car engine responded and I could drive the car without incident.

As I was driving, I felt nauseous and noticed the tiny hairs on my forearms were raised. The car felt much colder inside than before, even though no one had adjusted the air-conditioner.

Even though I was driving the car with no issues, Syifa did not stop crying. In fact, she was crying even louder than before. I concluded that she must have been scared of the 'Smurfs' cartoon that was being played on the DVD system. I glanced at the rearview mirror and saw that Syifa had cowered and buried her face to our maid's torso. Even though Wafa had changed the DVD to a different movie, Syifa continued crying. No matter how much Warsini tried to console Syifa, she did not stop crying until she fell asleep, whilst still in a tight embrace with our maid.

The next weekend Sunday, I brought Syifa for a mother-daughter grocery shopping day. I placed her in the child-car seat in the front passenger seat. Her child-car seat was quite adorable as it had its own toy steering wheel. Sometimes, I imagined that we were like 'Marge and Maggie' in the Simpsons animation show.

The strange thing was that even though Syifa was thrilled to go out with me, the moment I had placed her in her child-car seat, she looked very anxious and worried. She refused to look in the front and tried to hide her face on the side of the car seat. I did my best to ignore and drove the car.

We did not go far. Syifa was screaming at the top of her

voice and crying her eyes out.

I stopped the car at a nearby tuck-shop and released her seatbelt. The very moment I did that, she jumped onto my lap and hugged me tightly. She was shivering in fear. I brought her out of the car and into the shop. I tried my best to pacify her by buying a few trinkets and small cheap toys. Syifa calmed down, but when we approached the car, she embraced me tightly and refused to sit in her child-car seat.

I had no choice but to drive with her on my lap, hugging me ever so tightly. I know it was not the safest thing to do and I was worried someone would take a picture of me and post it on social media! Luckily, our house was nearby, so it was a very short drive.

When we got home, it took me a while to console and put her to sleep. All the while, I was thinking about what the cause of this really was. Suddenly, it dawned on me that she was not scared of the 'Smurfs' movie, but there must have been something at the front seat passenger side that had spooked her.

By chance, the next day at work, I met a friend of mine who practiced a registered form of religious healing. When I shared with her what had happened, she offered to help. She brought us to see an 'Ustaz' or religious officer at the 'Mufti' office. There the Ustaz performed a Ruqyah or religious eviction ritual on my daughter, whilst reading several Holy Verses directed at a bottle of water. He then asked Syifa to drink the blessed water.

My friend told me to collect water from one of the mosque's fountains and recite several Holy Verses and then sprinkle the water onto the car.

Additionally, I would recite Holy Verses from the Holy Book in my car. When I was alone in the car and felt calm and confident enough, I would speak out to the unseen entity, "Please leave my car and don't disturb my daughter. She's terrified of you. We don't want any trouble. Please leave."

Later on, after work, I would recite prayers for each of the corner of the car. Sometimes, I wondered how insane it sounded, especially to those who are unaware or do not believe in the unseen spirits, but I reminded myself of my daughter's reactions.

The next day I brought Syifa to the car. Initially, she had the same worried look on her face. However, when she sat down on my maid's lap, she looked around but did not cry. The next day I got her to sit in her child seat in the front passenger car-seat. She was not afraid; she was very calm.

I sighed a relief. Whatever it was, it was gone. Hopefully, it had not jumped into another car!

Dr Aammton Alias

The Banyan Tree

I had met Hamzah many years ago during a personal development course and we have kept in touch from time to time, especially when I visit his computer store. One day, I asked Hamzah if he had any ghost encounters - yes, it's a random question I ask from time to time - and initially he had stayed quiet. However, after I persisted, Hamzah turned out to have too many encounters. In hindsight, I should not have asked him.

When Hamzah was a child, he would be sent to his grandmother's house after school. His grandmother lived in a sturdy wooden stilted house and being the lone grandchild, he enjoyed the attention she was giving him. He was not just the golden child, but also the golden grandchild, so to say.

His grandmother would take long naps during the afternoon. With nothing else to do, Hamzah would wander off to the grassy backyard, doing his best to be near the huge wispy banyan tree. His grandmother warned him not to approach the banyan tree. Although Hamzah was only 7 years old then, he still thought his grandmother was merely being superstitious.

In the beginning, Hamzah would walk around the backyard and chase after small frogs and catch dragonflies. One time, being a callow lad, Hamzah tied a thin string round the end of a dragonfly and it would hover in mid-air as it tried to fly off. Hamzah gleed as he felt he had his own 'remote-control aircraft'.

"That is a cruel thing to do to that poor dragonfly! What if I tied you up and kept you near a monster? How would you feel about that?" Said a squeaky voice behind him.

Startled, Hamzah turned round to find three children standing behind him. The three of them, a boy and 2 girls, were of nearly the same height as Hamzah. They were of fair complexion, fairer than Hamzah, who some were convinced was almost Eurasian... almost. They were wearing colorful t-shirts and shorts, like he was. Hamzah noticed their clothes seemed brand new.

One girl had her arms crossed in disapproval. Without uttering a single word, the boy grabbed the dragonfly and quickly untied the string and let it flee to safety.

"Be free, dragonfly," He said and then turned to Hamzah, "You should not be cruel to God's creatures, no matter how small they may be."

"Who are you?" Hamzah was scared as he suddenly realised he was much nearer to the banyan tree than he remembered. Hamzah reasoned he must have gotten carried away with his dragonfly 'flying'.

"I'm Dilah, and these are my younger sisters, Darina and

Dinah. We live nearby," Dilah pointed to some houses in the distance, beyond his backyard and beyond another empty field.

"That's a bit far. I guess we are neighbours?" Hamzah concluded hesitantly.

"Yes, we are neighbours and to us, that is not far. We are used to walking 'far'. Anyway, Darina saw you and suggested we be friends with you. Shall we play a game of 'carah-duduk' since there's now four of us?" Carah-duduk is a local game of tag that involved squatting to remain 'safe'. It turned out Dinah, the youngest of the three, was the one with the crossed arms. She was wearing a new small t-shirt with a dragonfly artwork on it.

Hamzah's apprehension disappeared when they started their first game of carah-duduk. They had fun as they played in the backyard, laughing and giggling as they fell onto each other during their tag games. It was at this time that Hamzah apologized to Dinah for what he did to the dragonfly.

"Promise me you will never do that again!" Dinah insisted he made that promise, and when he did, she pinched his nose hard and then twisted it, "If you don't keep that promise, I will come after you!"

Hamzah tried his best to pinch her nose in retaliation,

but Dinah was agile and too slippery for him to grip.

Hamzah grew fond of his recent friends and every afternoon they would play all sort of games in the backyard, always making sure they keep their distance from the banyan tree. When it was nearly sunset, his friends would bid farewell and promise to meet up the next afternoon.

Hamzah watched them walk off towards the distant houses and he waved at them and they waved back.

Hamzah thought it was strange that his grandmother had not woken up yet. She was usually insistent that he was inside the house, well before sunset. She was a superstitious woman, after all. Hamzah had to wake his grandmother up, and when she got up, Hamzah's parents had just arrived from work.

They had dinner together and since it was Thursday evening i.e. the next day was not a working day for most civil servants; they had their usual sleepover at his grandmother's.

The sleepover would involve a small prayer recital function called the 'tahlil'. Usually, his uncles and aunts would join, but they all had their work commitments. This time it was just them four, and they didn't talk much even after dinner. Everyone was tired.

On Saturday, after school, Hamzah was dropped off at his grandmother's house. He was pretty excited to see his friends again. He didn't tell anyone at school about his newfound friends, as Hamzah did not have any actual friends in his school. He was not disliked by anyone but he did not know what to say and how to interact with his schoolmates, other than playing the frequent games they played at school.

Later that afternoon, when his grandmother was fast asleep, Hamzah went to his backyard and waited for his neighbours. He did not wait that long before Dilah, Darina and Dinah turned up in the backyard.

They played all afternoon, doing their best not to be too near the banyan tree. Hamzah noted that it was Darina who was the most cautious about getting close to the banyan tree.

At times, she would pause what she was doing and stare at the banyan tree. Dilah would also tap on her shoulder, startling her and getting her back into their rhythm of fun and games and their symphony of giggles and laughter. Before sunset, his three playmates would part ways and head home, promising to see the next day.

Hamzah enjoyed his afternoon fun for the next few weeks. They would talk about what they would do - the adventures they wish to set out to - when they got older. They talked about the favourite things they enjoyed and the things they feared.

One afternoon, Hamzah's mother came back from work early. It puzzled her on why Hamzah was not by the front door when she called out his name.

Something stirred inside, as though Hamzah was in danger. She looked around the house, but she could not find Hamzah. She went into Hamzah's grandmother's bedroom and found her in a deep sleep.

She had difficulty waking up Hamzah's grandmother. When she finally woke up, she immediately went back to sleep! Fearing the worst, Hamzah's mother ran out of the house and found Hamzah in the backyard.

Hamzah was playing with his friends. It relieved her to find her son well.

"Hamzah, come and greet your mother, and help me with the groceries I had bought," she hollered.

"But I want to play with my friends," Hamzah was not happy - he was the only child and he felt that he should not be made to do household chores.

"Hamzah, go to your mother. We are going home. We can play another time," Dilah was not too happy, but he did his best not to show any emotion. The three children walked away to their home.

Dr Aammton Alias

Real Ghost Stories of Borneo 4

Hamzah waved back to his friends, but this time they did not wave back. Hamzah was not happy with his mother. She had ruined a wonderful play afternoon.

Hamzah frowned all afternoon and all evening. He did not say a single word until his grandmother made his favourite 'bubur kacang' or sweet bean porridge.

"Hamzah, who are the children you are playing with in my backyard?"

"Three siblings named Dilah, Darina and Dinah. They live in one of the houses across the field, so that makes us neighbours."

"Ah yes, I remember that family. Mr. Daud, the widower and his three children."

Hamzah's mother sighed in relief, "I thought Hamzah was playing gho…"

Hamzah's father stopped her mid-sentence, as it was not good to cause a jinx in the evening.

The next afternoon, Hamzah waited for his friends Dilah, Darina and Dinah. He waited for hours, but they did not turn up. He waited until sunset, when his parents were there to pick him up.

Hamzah was feeling glum. He wondered why his friends were not turning up. Perhaps his mother had looked at them a bit too sternly.

Hamzah's friends did not turn up for many afternoons after that.

One day after school, Hamzah asked his mother to drive him to his friends' house.

"What if their parents don't want them to be out all afternoon? If you play out in the hot sun, you could get sick," she was not keen to go as she did not want to be late for her afternoon shift. But her will was not as strong as Hamzah's and she finally caved in.

She drove her car to where Hamzah pointed out to and found several dilapidated stilted huts. The wood had rotten through, and beams were broken in many places and were falling apart.

Some huts were so tiny they looked more like abandoned rice grain store huts instead of accommodations. The grass was so overgrown, she could not drive close into the area.

She had goosebumps all over, and every instinct of hers told her not to go further or she will lose more than her life. She felt as though they were being watched by the Unseen.

Real Ghost Stories of Borneo 4

"I am sure they are hiding somewhere here," Hamzah did not understand what was happening and wanted to get to the bottom of it all. His mother immediately locked the car and sped away as fast as she could.

It was lucky that she did not hit an incoming truck on the main road. Fearing for their safety, she did not bother to go to Hamzah's grandmother's house. Hamzah had to be by her side in her office all afternoon.

The next day, she took the day off and brought Hamzah to his grandmother's house. Hamzah's mother was almost hysterical when she shared about what had happened.

"The Daud family are good-hearted spirits. They have lived there long before your grandfather was here. I used to play with them myself when I was a child. They won't harm us. They even protect us from the others."

Hamzah's mother froze in terror when she heard those words from his grandmother.

Hamzah was forbidden from playing in the backyard, but there was no one to actually stop him from going to the backyard. He tried to walk to where the abandoned houses were but found the grass in the adjacent field to be too tall and too daunting for him.

Every afternoon, he would sit down in the grassy backyard, regardless of whether the sun was blazing hot, or if it was raining heavily. His friends never turned up.

One afternoon, Hamzah felt sorry for himself and cried. He promised himself that this would be the last time he would wait for them. Upon making that promise, he quickly fell asleep in the grass, still sobbing. Hamzah was woken up suddenly by a familiar face. It was Darina!

"Wake up, it's already sunset, you must get back in. Hurry!" She pulled Hamzah up and pushed him.

"Why? Where's Dilah and Dinah? We can play in grandmother's house!"

"No, Hamzah. We can't. You must hurry. Go now!" There was a sense of great distress and urgency in Darina's voice.

It was then Hamzah saw ominous shadows emerge from the banyan tree; the shadows merged into a shape as tall as the towering tree itself, and the shape morphed into a faceless humanoid figure.

"Run, Hamzah!" Hamzah sprinted as fast as he could to his grandmother's house as the tall shadow demon chased after him. His legs could only take him as fast as humanly possible; he had no chance of outrunning a giant demon.

He sensed the demon was catching up to him, and in that moment, a cold, giant claw-like hand grabbed his shoulder. Hamzah screamed as he found himself being propelled backwards. He fell to the ground and knew this was the moment he would be taken. He had heard of tales of children disappearing without a trace and he thought this was how it had happened.

Instead, someone pulled him up in the nick of time, it was Dinah. Her brother Dilah was there too and he was doing his best to obstruct the demon.

"Get home, NOW!" Dilah and Dinah yelled out, as they too began to retreat. But not before Dinah was able to give a firm push to Hamzah who ran with every ounce of his life towards safety.

He jumped on to a flight of wooden steps and then bolted through the house doors. As he turned his back to close the doors, he could see the giant legs of the demon walk over the house. Hamzah ran into his grandmother's bedroom and furiously woke her up.

"Hamzah, you are safe with me. You are safe in this house," She consoled him. Hamzah had difficulty sleeping that night, having screaming terrors all night long. His parents had to sleep with him and they had to leave the lights on. This went on for several weeks.

Hamzah never waited in the backyard after that, but sometimes when he gazed from the window of the house on rainy afternoons, he could see Darina waving back at him from the backyard.

When he wanted to meet her, she gestured with her hands not to leave the house. Although he could not hear her words, he felt Darina and the others had harbored no ill feelings and were looking out for him.

Hamzah found out later that the towering shadow demon was an 'orang tinggi' demon. It was not the last time that he had seen and encountered the orang tinggi demon.

Even today, Hamzah still sleeps with the light on.

A Raya Story

I wondered if Hadi was avoiding me. Did I do anything wrong? I was keen to meet up with Hadi. For some reason, Hadi had been busy, and he didn't have time to spend with me. It was the second day of 'Hari Raya Aidilfitri'. He should be home.

I don't remember what year it was, but it was definitely back in the early 1980s, 1 or 2 years before our country's Independence Day. I assume it was 1982 or 1983. I suppose those were the only things I could remember. Watching the news clips of a war in the Falkland Islands, to which at the age of 5 or 6 years old, I could not comprehend. The news seemed exciting at that time. I learnt later in life that is how the tragedy of war will always be portrayed as.

The other significant thing I remembered at that age was our National Independence Day in 1984. Again, at 5 - 6 years old, I had no idea what it meant, but everyone my age recalled where they were during the Independence celebration-declaration.

Anyway, I lived with my grandmother in Serusop and I was close with my neighbours, especially Hadi and his younger brother, Helmi. Helmi was actually the same age as me and he was at one time my closest friend, if not my best friend back then. Hadi was around 10 years older. Hadi was the big brother I never had. I looked up to him, and I associated everything he did as being cool and awesome. He had curly hair, which reminded me of that famous Malaysian band called Alleycats. Both Hadi and Helmi were full of energy, funny and playful.

I had spent most of my days after school at their place. However, I had not seen Hadi or Helmi for several days and I was missing them. Raya was a time to celebrate, and I was sure they would be there in their home.

I asked my mother to let me wear yesterday's baju raya with my 'sinjang' - a Malay version of the kilt and put on my 'songkok' (traditional Malay hat). She asked me why. I told her I was going next door to see Hadi and Helmi. My mother pinched her lower lip with her thumb and index finger. It was a strange habit she had. Then she said, "Sure, but you better ask for permission from your father first."

I went into the living room where I found my father talking to my granduncle and uncles. I was too excited to be polite and ended up interrupting their lively conversation.

"Dad, can I go to Hadi's and Helmi's house next door?"

Everyone in the room was silent, and the silence seemed to grow louder and louder with every passing second. It made me wonder if our family had a fight with the neighbours. My father stared at me and eventually concluded that I had nothing to do with the grown-up world.

"Alright son, but don't stay there for too long."

With that, I rushed back to my mother and changed my clothes.

Back in the 1980s, there was nothing wrong about unaccompanied young children walking on their own across the backyard forest to their neighbour's house. No one had thought about the dangers of child abduction, even though there was enough Disney cartoons on children being kidnapped.

I strolled across the grassy path through the half cleared and yet lush green forest towards Hadi's house. The morning dew was still clinging to the grass blades, so I had to walk slowly, doing my best not to taint my baju Melayu trousers. It was already hard enough to get rid of the hitchhiker grass seeds, let alone the dirt.

By the time I got to Hadi's house, it surprised me there were not that many people visiting his house. Like my family, Hadi's parents, his uncles, his aunts and his grandfather lived in the same house. This was common back then, where the whole extended family was living under one roof.

I could only see a single car that I did not recognise. I walked into the house giving my Raya Aidilfitri greeting. I had expected to see the house packed with visitors. Instead, in the corner of the wide and spacious living room, I saw Hadi's eldest brother, Hassan, talking to his brother-in-law, whom I did not recognise.

This stranger had only recently gotten married to Hadi's sister, so that made him the new brother-in-law. They both looked at me, and smiled and then ignored me, continuing what seemed to be a serious conversation.

I suppose at 5-6 years old, I was pretty goal-orientated; I came to them and kissed their hands, greeting them again. I had no understanding of the impertinence of interrupting serious discussion between adults.

I asked Hadi's eldest brother, Hassan, if Hadi and Helmi were at home. His response was at first seemingly stern. He looked very serious, and I wondered if he wanted to scold me. I should not have interrupted them. I hoped he would not give me a good telling off. Perhaps it was because I was my father's only child, so 'Abang' Hassan thought twice about scolding me.

The brother-in-law shrugged his shoulders and suddenly made babbling sounds, moving his hands ungracefully in the air, basically pretending to be a mute.

"Why would you do that? I just saw you talk with Abang

Real Ghost Stories of Borneo 4

Hassan! You are not mute."

Hassan did his best to keep himself composed, whilst the brother-in-law continued with his act. Making babbling sounds and muffled noises, he continued his act. It got me upset that he was trying to outsmart me. I tried giving him 'Salam greetings' expecting a compulsory response, but he merely made a muted response. I kept on playing, challenging him several times, and eventually I laughed out loud.

I noticed their similarities. Both Hassan and the 'new' guy sported rather thin moustaches, unlike my clean-shaven father.

"What is 'uncle's name?" I asked him. I had to call him 'uncle' as both Hassan and he were as old as my father.

"I'm Uncle Hamdan," he chuckled, and then added, "Sometimes, I can't speak."

"Oh, come on, I am too smart for that," I replied confidently.

"Uncle, do you know where Abang Hadi and Helmi are?"

There was a lengthy pause before Abang Hassan answered, "Helmi is in his room. Maybe busy playing."

I wondered if they were hiding something from me. I will

get to the bottom of this soon, I assured myself. Everybody seemed to be doing their best to ignore me today, but I will persist. "I am the most persistent!" I vowed to myself.

Both Helmi's and Hadi's rooms were upstairs. As I was quite accustomed to going to their rooms, I made my way down the hallway towards the kitchen where Hadi's mother was busy squatting and pounding the pestle into the mortar. I can only assume 'Nenek Auntie' as I would call her, was preparing chilli sambal paste.

I greeted her but her back was facing me; she did not reply and I decided to leave her to her own device. I ran up the stairs towards Helmi's room. His room was the closest to the staircase.

I knocked on the door a few times, but no one answered. I called out Helmi's name a few times, but there was no answer. I was sure he was inside, as I could hear rummaging. "It's Raya today. Why is everyone avoiding me?" I shouted aloud and opened the door.

Sure enough, Helmi was there. He was playing alone in the room with his toy cars.

"Selamat Hari Raya Aidilfitri! Maaf Zahir dan Batin!" My voice boomed and echoed in his room. I expected Helmi to jump up and give me a warm embrace and then we would try to lift each other up whilst in our bear hug mode. This was something we would usually do, our own signature greeting.

However, Helmi said nothing. He did not even bother to face me. Helmi continued on pushing his small toy car up a ramp and then letting it fall. He kept on doing this repeatedly.

I called out to him a few times, and since he said nothing, I went up close to him and put my hand on his shoulder. No response.

It was as though I was not there.

"Helmi, this isn't funny. This is Raya, I don't like this prank you are playing."

Helmi continued to ignore me, and I wondered if this was really Helmi. Maybe he is a -I did my best to pause my mind from coming up with the conclusion but to no avail - a ghost.

Deciding enough was enough, I grabbed the toy car from Helmi's hand and hurled it to the corner of the room.

Helmi shouted at me, "Get out! I don't want to see you again!"

It shocked me, as I had never seen this angry side of

Helmi before. It scared me, as Helmi was always the funny and fun-going friend. I ran out of the room, holding back my tears.

"What did I do wrong?" I said to myself.

It was at this moment that I saw a silhouette in the corner of my eye. It was Hadi, and he was entering his room.

I ran towards his room, "Abang Hadi, Selamat Hari Raya Aidilfitri! Wait!"

Hadi had either ignored me or he did not hear me. This is so annoying. What is wrong with everyone?

I knocked on his door twice, but as I was no longer patient with everyone, I flung open the door.

"Abang Hadi, Selamat Hari Raya Aidilfitri!" To my surprise there was no one in the room. I was sure Hadi had gone into his room. I noticed his room seemed neat. Organised and tidied, this was not usual. Even his acoustic guitar was in its stand instead of his chair.

"Where are you hiding, I wonder?" I said it out loud so that Hadi could hear me. He must be hiding somewhere in the room.

I quickly crouched and looked under the bed. There was no one there. I flung open the closet and yelled out,

Real Ghost Stories of Borneo 4

"Gotcha!" The closet was full of his clothes and other belongings, but he was not there.

What's going on?

I sat on his bed and felt very sad about how my second day of Raya Aidilfitri was not turning out to be the way I had expected. I went up to Hadi's guitar and plucked a few strings. I wish I could play the guitar the way Abang Hadi did. He would serenade a few Malay slow rock love songs outside the house, and I thought he was a talented singer, especially when he played the Alleycats songs. People would comment on how he looked like the lead singer of the Alleycats. I hummed a melody from one of his favourite Alleycats songs. It was then that I noticed that there was a light flowery scent in the room. I guess Abang Hadi was wearing perfume now, perhaps he has got a special friend who is not a boy i.e. a girlfriend.

With nothing left to do, I decided I should go home. Nobody wanted to play with me. As I walked out of Hadi's room, I was sure Hadi was inside. I looked back, but he was not there. With a heavy heart, I trudged down the stairs, each step getting heavier and heavier.

By the time I got down the stairs, I felt a warm and tight embrace. It wasn't Hadi. It was Nenek Auntie. It was not her usual embrace, as it was a long and silent hug. Her head was on top of my head, and my hair was becoming moist. I could feel Nenek Auntie trembling as she whispered, "Selamat Hari Raya Aidilfitri. Be a smart, good and helpful man when you grow up, okay?"

She handed me an orange $10 note, with no green packet to conceal it. $10 back then was like getting a $100 note, which was amazing.

I was overjoyed and thanked her. I noticed how she tried her best not to show her face to me. For an instant, I had forgotten all my sorrows and made my way home.

It was only when I got home that I cried. Both Hadi and Helmi had ignored me. My mother came up to me and asked what had happened. I explained how both Abang Hadi and Helmi had ignored me. She seemed startled when I told her how I was sure Abang Hadi was hiding inside the room somewhere.

She kissed my head and hugged me. "Son, Abang Hadi had an accident a few weeks ago. A car had slammed into his motorbike," she paused, "Do you remember?"

"Mama, how come I don't remember you telling me that? Is he in the hospital?"

"No, Abang Hadi broke his neck when a car hit his motorbike. He died instantly." My mother made the decision not to tell me that she had already told me this a number of times.

Real Ghost Stories of Borneo 4

I pondered upon the meaning of dying instantly and then I asked my mother, "When will he be back?"

My mother tried her best to explain that death was a path of no return. Even then, I did not understand the meaning of death and demise. There were times I would cry in bed upon realising that I would not see Hadi again. He had disappeared from the face of the world, at least my world. I never had a chance to say goodbye, let alone spend another Raya with him.

Helmi and I drifted apart, as going to his house reminded me of the loss of Hadi. What compounded matters was that we never ever mentioned his name there or anything or any memory that was related to him. We were a trio, and without Hadi, things were not the same. Eventually my parents found their own place, and we moved out of my grandmother's house.

From time to time, especially during Raya Aidilfitri, I would remember Hadi and all the friends and family members that are no longer with us. When I hear that song "*Andainya Aku Pergi Dulu*" from Alleycats, which somehow always makes it into the Raya Aidilfitri playlist, I would remember him. I would end up reflecting upon our lives and re-evaluate what is truly important to us, which is to live our moments as true to ourselves and be close to those whom we cherish.

The Residents

Original story contributed by Firah

I could only see his nose and his eyes, if it was a 'he' at all. It was more of an 'it' but deep inside I knew this ghost was a he...

My late father used to work as a diplomat, which meant my family was always outside of the country. Whenever we returned to our home country, which was once or twice a year, we would stay at our grandparents' house. We did not have our own house.

My grandparents' house was in Bunut village. During that time, Bunut was a sleepy village; it was not yet developed into the sprawling suburb that it is now. The house was an old house, renovated to accommodate changes in the family.

It was initially a wooden stilted house, but my grandfather had an extension on the ground floor, hence cement was used for the ground floor whilst the walls of the rooms were made with modern bricks and mortar, with modern windows.

Not wanting to lose the original aspects of his house, my grandfather kept the first floor in its original state, i.e. wooden. It would probably look like a strange concept now these days, but back then in the 1980s and 90s, it was a trending adaptation.

I loved coming home to my grandparents. The Damuan river was behind the house. When we were bored, we would always watch the river. Of course, I would never recommend anyone to swim in it as there were most likely crocodiles lurking beneath the green waters of the gentle meandering river.

My father's relatives used to live in the house next door. They were unlike the usual neighbours, as they kept to themselves, and rarely came out to greet us. Somehow, my grandparents were very comfortable with that.

My aunt or 'Angah' lived with my grandparents and she had the largest room. When we were there, my 3 elder brothers and myself would sleep in her room. We would have these roll-up mattresses and place them on the floor before going to sleep. That was the arrangement we had, and hence we got close to our *angah*.

You could say the household was very much lively and noisy as there were many of us under one roof and we were true chatterboxes.

However, during the evenings, especially after sunset or 'maghrib' time, I had an uneasy feeling in my chest. The fact that the house was poorly lit at night did not help.

The upstairs fluorescent light had dimmed a long time ago, and my grandparents promised to replace it once it burned out, but it never did. It would flicker on and off, permanently at Death's door but never giving up its light. When you thought it was gone, the white fluorescent tubes would suddenly brighten up, but almost barely.

Sometimes, I wish they would just replace the damned bulbs, especially the ones above the upstairs toilet and the corridor between my parents and my grandmother's rooms.

I tried to shake off the nocturnal uneasiness because I was not superstitious and I did not really believe in ghosts. Even as a child, I would say it privileged me as a diplomat's child that I had seen more of the world than most children of my age in my country.

And yet, I felt goosebumps and a chill going down my spine. Every evening, with no reasonable explanation, I felt someone, or something was looking at me from outside the first-floor corridor window.

It did not help that this particular window had no curtains. As much as I tried to fight the feeling, and as much as I tried to reason that there was nothing to be afraid of, every bit of me was scared for my life.

I did my best not to look at the window. The more I resisted, the more I could not stop myself, as though my

Real Ghost Stories of Borneo 4

body gravitated towards it. When I glanced at the window, I would quickly turn my head away from it, and in the corner of my eye, I could see a shadowy figure at the window. I wanted to believe that it was a figment of my imagination, but that would mean I would have to look at the window again and confront the notion that there was something there. I never had the courage to look at it again.

Sometimes I would tell my parents what had happened. They would tell me to ignore it and recite my prayers to ward off any evil spirits.

I decided it was best that I just run past the corridor window when I was alone at night. By right, that should have been the end, but it wasn't.

One late evening, I was lying down on my floor mattress in my angah's bedroom. I wasn't alone. My angah was fast asleep on her bed, which was next to me, whilst my brothers were doing their usual stay-up-all-night routine, playing their PlayStation 2 game console in one corner of the bedroom. I could not sleep; something was keeping me awake.

It was not my brothers' game-playing; I could sleep through that easily. I wasn't sure what it was. I was turning on my side and hoping I would fall asleep, but I didn't. I tried lying on my tummy, but that didn't help either.

For some unknown reason, by instinct, I looked up towards the bedroom window. This window had a set of curtains, so it was safe, and yet I looked up, almost expectantly.

At first, I was numb. I saw something, and I did not believe it. I rubbed my face onto my pillow and looked up again.

The end of the window curtains was being pulled up. The window was definitely closed, so it could not be the wind. As I squinted in disbelief, I saw the end of the curtains being pulled a quarter of the way up, and there it stared at me.

I wanted to scream, cry and run, but I could not. I was frozen in time. I had to wake up my angah and get her and myself out of harm's way. Then it struck that no one else was seeing this but me.

It stared at me and I stared back, as though hypnotised by its presence. What was it? I kept asking myself. Its face looked human and yet I could only see his soft enormous nose and large red eyes, everything else about its features was a big blur, a shape that I could barely see.

I felt myself in great danger, my heart pounding hard, and yet I could not escape from harm's way. Our eyes locked onto each other for what seemed like an eternity, whilst it decided upon my fate.

Eventually, I could blink again, and then I quickly buried my face onto my pillow and uttered a prayer verse. With all my courage, I looked up again to the window where it was. It was no longer there.

The window was not open, and the curtains had not been pulled back. It was not there anymore. I wept there whilst muffling my sobs with my pillow. I wanted to tell someone, but I was terrified it would come back if I talked that very evening.

I jumped onto my angah's bed and tightly hugged my angah, who was still fast asleep.

I could not forget it, I could not unsee what I had seen. The image had been seared into my mind. Although I could only see the nose and the red eyes. I somehow knew it was a 'he'. What I had seen was more of an 'it' but deep inside I knew this ghost was a male entity.

Somehow I fell asleep, whilst still sobbing and sweating in fear.

My angah woke me up in the morning. It surprised her to see me sleeping next to her.

When I told her what had happened, she dismissed it

nonchalantly.

"Don't worry, this is 'his' house too. He just wants to show himself as you are an unfamiliar person to this house. You know, like guests. Everyone greets their guests, right?" My angah's explanation seemed straightforward and yet it wasn't. At least not to me.

I was not even sure if my angah was trying to pacify me with a calming story. I had no doubt that I had felt clear and present danger during the incident.

After breakfast, I confronted my angah and told her I was not sure if I believed her. That was when her confession came out.

She told me she had seen a lot of other 'people' in the house. She had also seen a lady spirit in the house along with dwarf-like male spirits, and 'orang tinggi' demons outside the house.

She said she got used to it, and there was nothing to be afraid of, as 'they' would not bother us as long as we did not bother them. Somewhere along the line, she uttered, "We live in a shared world. We just have to get along with each other somehow."

Strangely enough, I never had another direct spiritual encounter, for which I am grateful for. I still have that occasional uneasiness, the feeling someone was

Real Ghost Stories of Borneo 4

watching me.

My brothers had often gotten unwell after seeing the supernatural beings. They would often share with me what they saw, and it was just like what my angah had mentioned: there was a lady spirit in the house along with dwarf-like male spirits, and 'orang tinggi' demons roaming outside the house, especially after dark.

Many years later, I shared my encounter with my grandmother. She told me it was not a resident of her house; the insidious demon was from next door and she pointed to the abandoned rundown house next door. Our former neighbours.

Dr Aammton Alias

The New Job Challenges

Original story contributed by Wilhelm aka Mr. M, written by Erica Aammton.

As somebody who was about to start their first day with a new job, I was very excited. I went to bed early, hoping for a fresh start on the big day. However, my brain would not power down as I kept on thinking about the new things I would experience, such as meeting new colleagues, having work parties, showing how efficient I would be at work and what to do with my first salary.

The next day, even with only 5 hours of sleep, I was up bright and early. I arrived at the office one hour before the office was officially open. There were very few people at the office: two security officers, another colleague who was also starting his first day into a new job and the manager who told us that there will be a short briefing later for the new staff.

Since it was still early and there was not much to do, the manager told us to wait outside his office on the large red leather sofa until the rest of the new staff had arrived. While waiting, I happily chatted with my new colleague.

The room was chilly, and we were visibly shivering as none of us had brought sweaters. It is a hot tropical country so sweaters would always be the last thing on our minds to bring. Despite the cold, we did not move out of the room. Instead, we sat down chatting quietly, our voices visibly shaking. The blazing tropical climate made us very grateful for the air-conditioner, no matter how we felt.

Naturally, the frigid temperature allowed us to become best friends with the toilets. Before the briefing started, I had already used the toilet about three times. It did not help that I had cereal and an enormous cup of tea for breakfast before I left my house this morning. The only unnatural thing about the toilet was that it was slightly dim and once in a while the fluorescent lights would flicker for a few seconds.

The office washroom have been designed in such a standard way in public toilets i.e. the mirrors and sinks had been installed on one side whilst five toilet cubicles were on the opposite side of the room.

The mirror facing the middle cubicle had a gigantic crack in it. I was told by a colleague who was here longer that the crack originated from some children who thought it was a good idea to play ball here. The manager considered replacing the mirror as not a priority and had not been replaced since.

After the short briefing, I had another urge to use the toilet again as the central air conditioning system was powerful and I was still shivering at the desk during the whole briefing session.

Just as I was about to flush the toilet, water suddenly gushed into the toilet bowl. It had flushed itself. For the first three times I had gone, I manually flushed it. Most people would probably freak out and run away if this happened to them, but all I could think about was: Oh nice, this toilet is an automatic toilet. No supernatural-related thoughts entered my head, and I did not bother to check if the toilet was automatic or not. Furthermore, I was in a different toilet cubicle compared to the previous three times.

Later, I asked one of my older colleagues how many automatic toilets the company had installed in this building. There was a half-minute pause as he looked at me blankly and then replied:

"None of our toilets are automatic."

He then asked me why I would ask such a question, so I told him that the toilet in the cubicle that was the farthest away from the door had flushed itself after I used it.

"People rarely use that cubicle for a reason. Next time, if you need to use it and it flushes by itself, just ignore it and carry on with your life as best as you can."

He then walked away.

Real Ghost Stories of Borneo 4

I became quite spooked after that. Ever since that day, my paranoia increased tenfold. I never wanted to be the last one in the office when work ends.

Other than the toilet, I found my overall work experience to be pleasant. The office had nice soft carpeting covering the whole floor right up to the toilets, the pantry and all doors leading outside the building. They felt very heavenly under my feet. However, it can be a pain to clean, which was why shoes were not allowed into the office.

One day, as I entered the building, I could hear a lot of voices coming from the main office area. I saw the cleaners and some other staff pointing at the carpet. On the carpet, there were a lot of dry muddy footprints going from the toilet and crossing the middle of the main office area. The footprints stopped before a set of double doors that led to a dressing room of a nearby hall.

The footprints were small, so everybody present immediately deduced that they belonged to a child. However, nobody here had brought any children with them. We knew that the manager had brought his children here the day before.

However, they stayed in his office the whole time and we would have noticed all these footprints. Furthermore, the manager and his children left earlier, before any of us. We also concluded that it could not be any naughty school children as it was just before 8am on a school day and the cleaners had found the footprints at 7am.

As everybody argued and theorised with one another, I noticed the cleaners were whispering with each other.

Curiously, I asked them about their opinions regarding this matter. One of them replied quietly with only one word and a pale face: "Hantu" which means ghost in English. Another said that it could be Pontianak or "little spirits". She too said this in a quiet voice.

One of the staff who held a top position and had an arrogant personality overheard our conversation. He laughed aloud and openly belittled the cleaners for believing in superstitions. The cleaners immediately told him to keep his voice down as they were afraid the spirits could hear him and to avoid 'cabul'.

Instead of listening to them, he turned and started walking around the main office area, calling out to the spirits to do their worst to him as he did not believe they existed.

After a few minutes, he stopped and looked at the cleaners with a smug grin on his face.

Real Ghost Stories of Borneo 4

Mysterious footsteps @krkdile

He then opened his mouth after a while but whatever he was going to say never came out because at that moment, the double doors of the dressing room suddenly slammed open and a strong gust of wind came into the office, causing papers from a nearby pile to go flying about the room.

As suddenly as the doors opened, they slammed shut with a deafening slam. Immediately, the senior staff's face turned pale whereas one look at the cleaners' faces was all I needed to confirm what I also thought: Hantu.

But the supernatural beings were not done with their work.

On that same day while I was working at my desk, sorting out important documents, I suddenly heard coins falling onto the carpet from a tall place. I ignored it, expecting the person who dropped them to pick them up.

It seemed nobody did because fifteen minutes later, I heard someone shout out in Malay, "Who dropped their coins? Even if it is only 5 cents, you should not throw them away!" The shouting echoed throughout the whole office area.

A few heads popped out of their cubicles while a few "nope, not me" could be heard from other nearby cubicles. I also looked out to see whose voice it was.

Standing in the middle whilst holding a stack of multi-coloured files was Johnny, the 'company clown'. He had picked up the coins and announced that he would take the coins if nobody claimed them.

I got up and greeted him, telling him I heard someone dropping coins not so long ago. He merely replied that since nobody wanted them, he might as well take them to add to his own savings. It was strange that somebody would leave the coins on the carpet. Sure, it was in small denominations, but you don't just throw money away! If it was by accident, the person who dropped it should be able to hear it.

This happened a few more times in random places. Sometimes the coins would fall on to a table before rolling down onto the carpet. Nobody knew who dropped them, but the sound each time was loud enough to make us all think they were falling from the ceiling.

Johnny had suggested that we might have an old chest full of treasure in the ceilings and that rats above our heads were playing around, causing the chest to pour coins. This theory was immediately debunked as the coins had been falling in random places and were found to be minted recently.

Nobody wanted to climb a ladder and check the ceiling as we were afraid of seeing something undesirable like in the horror movies. This was understandable since everybody here had experienced a form of supernatural presence.

After a few weeks, we held a prayer ceremony in the office. We put a few 'Surah Yassin' books in the few windows that the building had. All supernatural acts suddenly vanished after that day, and until now we do not have a plausible explanation as to why these events happened.

Camping at the Beach

Original story written by 'Sabri'.

It was late at night. I was already asleep when my phone chimed loudly. An unexpected WhatsApp message from a lawyer friend of mine alarmed me. I was wondering if it was a scandal that was unfolding or some medicolegal work opportunity for me. To my disappointment, it was neither. My lawyer friend was a fan of my book and shared with me a Reddit post about some guy having had a supernatural encounter at Tungku beach. I dismissed it as the source of the story was not someone I knew. It could have been a bored student from an international school who wanted some excitement in his life, by creating fake drama, fake news.

A few months later, I found out the person who made that Reddit post was the brother of a good friend of mine, and he was no bored school kid. Sabri was a local businessman and ran a martial arts dojo or school. Instead of expecting a student, I was met by a martial arts sensei.

Sabri had an outstanding student named Rashid, whom he was grooming to be a martial arts instructor. During their discussion, they concluded they should set up a bonding program for new instructors and keen students.

To hold an annual retreat would be something that would elevate the status of the dojo. Sabri had heard certain dojos in other countries had done something similar. However, they had strong bonds between the guru and the second in charge instructor.

Rashid suggested that the two of them try camping first and see how it progressed. The plan would be to eventually get the other instructors to join in the camping sessions. However, Sabri did not want to camp in the middle of the jungle.

"Let's try somewhere nearby first," Sabri insisted.

"How about Tungku beach?" Rashid pointed out it was safe, very accessible as it was next to the main highway and it was easy to leave from. Mobile phone reception was also very good, especially if there were any unlikely emergencies.

They decided Friday evening would be the best time to camp at Tungku beach. They would have preferred to camp on Thursday night, but there was a local belief that ghosts were more likely to appear on Thursday night.

The following Friday afternoon, the duo drove to Tungku beach, a sandy outcrop lined and protected with wave-resistant formation of quarry rocks. They chose a site that was nearest to the path towards the sandy beach area. The place was on a higher plane, protected by quarry rocks. They could easily walk down to the sandy beach to have a quick swim, wash their hands, etc.

They set up camp and noted it was eerily quiet. They had expected a few other campers to be around, but no one else was there.

Whilst preparing the campfire, a middle-aged man with a worn out blue t-shirt and sneakers approached them. They did not understand how he managed to sneak up to them without them noticing.

The softly spoken man introduced himself as Yahya, and he was the watchman for Tungku beach. He told them they were not supposed to be camping at the beach. The beach was not for the public after hours. Camping was forbidden.

However, Sabri and Rashid insisted they had a right to camp there. Yahya asked them if they would consume any intoxicating items i.e. alcohol and drugs. The question initially shocked Sabri and Rashid, but they quickly concluded this was probably from the watchman's past experience.

Yahya initially demanded they set up camp somewhere else as this was a terrible spot. To which Rashid explained that it was the safest and most convenient place to camp.

After much persuasion with Yahya, they convinced him they were not budging and they would not be trouble for him. Yahya raised his hands in surrender and warned them that if the authorities were to do a spot inspection, then it would be their responsibility, as he had already warned them several times.

The campfire was blazing, and it was already 'Maghrib'. They had their ablution with the seawater and then proceeded to pray together.

After prayers, Sabri reflected upon their day and felt quite impressed with their campsite. They had a nice campfire going and a modern camp, which was a clam-like tent with a single exit. It did not need to be secured or slung to a tree and was weatherproof.

They had cooked a nice red snapper fish, which Rashid had purchased from the nearby Jerudong fish market.

Sitting round the campfire, the two talked about the inner mysteries of 'Tarekan' or inner energy in their martial arts practice. He enjoyed Rashid's company and realised he would make an excellent leader amongst his students.

Without warning, Sabri felt a firm tap on his shoulder. He was facing Rashid, so he knew it could not have been him. He turned around immediately and saw there was no one on the deserted Tungku beach behind them.

Real Ghost Stories of Borneo 4

Sabri had no doubt he felt the tap on his shoulder. It felt very real. His mind raced to the one conclusion and colour drained from his face. Sabri said nothing of it, and tried to continue the lively conversation, but stumbled with his words.

Rashid immediately noticed the disturbed, worrisome look on his master's face. Choosing not to 'cabul' or jinx the situation, Rashid picked up his mobile phone and sent a message to Sabri, to enquire what was going on.

It was strange that two grown men sitting by a campfire were sending each other mobile phone messages, when they were only two meters away from each other.

"Everything is fine," Sabri messaged back. Sabri did not want to cause any panic and was sure this was the end of the incident. Eventually, Sabri picked up from where they left their last conversation and forgot about the mysterious shoulder tap.

After dinner and 'Isyak' prayers, the two men called it a night and went to sleep inside their tent. As the fish they had eaten was bigger than usual, the both of them fell asleep, satiated.

Around 1am, Sabri was awakened by what he first thought was a low tone rumbling. Sabri listened intently. It was not a rumbling. It was a soft but constant growl.

He checked on Rashid, believing that he was snoring, but Rashid was wide awake and trying to figure out the source of the uninvited sound.

"Master, can you hear that... growling?" whispered Rashid, who by right had already known the answer to his question.

Sabri nodded in response.

The growling went on and it sounded very near. Their hearts raced; their breathing became shallow in anticipation of an 'attack. Rashid trembled in fear. Just when they thought they were in a rut, it had gotten worse. A high-pitched, echoing cackling preceded the long growling. They could not pinpoint where the cackling was coming from exactly, as though it was coming from all directions and yet nowhere. They both knew the word to describe the sound, 'Mengilai' which was a typical description of the cackling from a Pontianak vampire!

Sabri and Rashid were stuck in the tent and contemplated on the action plan. They were both fighters. They couldn't just let this slip pass by them. Before either could formulate a plan, a gentle scratching on the side of the tent, interrupted their thoughts. It was like a fingernail that was dragging itself slowly against the fabric of the tent.

Real Ghost Stories of Borneo 4

Sabri asked himself, "Should we get out and confront it? What if one of us gets compromised or possessed?"

It was at that moment that an exit strategy was the right move.

They decided it was a terrible idea to continue camping. They both thought it was better to head home. They will confront the Pontianak, strike its head with all their might! But no matter what happens, the primary plan was to get to the car!

Rashid trembled in fear and was hesitant. Sabri was not having any of that from his star pupil, a future instructor.

"Man up!" shouted Sabri.

And with that, Sabri and Rashid leapt out of their tent, with their own battle cries, arms and legs in combat stance, ready to strike their more likely overpowering nemesis. Yet their prowess display had no apparent guest.

Sabri noticed a strangeness of the night. He was dumbstruck, or to be precise, moonstruck. The night was surreal, probably the most beautiful night in his life. It did not make much sense as this was 'only' Tungku beach.

The most obvious abnormality was a full moon in the

night sky. He was sure it was not supposed to be a full moon that night. The moon seemed much brighter and much closer than usual. The moonlight lit a part of the beach and the sea nearby, reflecting a shimmer on the sea surface. The sea was so calm it looked like a canvas. It did not seem real. The air was much cooler than before, and there was no wind blowing, which was not typical of Tungku beach.

On any other occasion, it would have been the setting for a perfect romantic evening. The eeriness of it made Sabri wonder if this was another world, a crossing of the spiritual world and our world. They had to leave.

The two men took their valuables but left the tent as they planned to take it back the next day. They headed cautiously to their car. They expected the Pontianak to be there, waiting for its moment to pounce on them! That's how it always was in the horror movies. When they got to the car, they both felt goosebumps, and they knew they were being watched.

"Get ready for it," Sabri whispered. However, to their relief, the Pontianak did not appear.

Rashid wondered if they could move to where the other campers were, or 'take refuge'. Surely some other people must be camping there too. Yet, they looked like the only souls on the beach.

Real Ghost Stories of Borneo 4

Nevertheless, they got in the car and drove slowly on the sandy beach, looking for signs of other people, but no one else was there.

Giving up, they decided it was best to leave the beach and head home. They will sort out everything else the next day.

However, when they went to the exit, the gate had been shut and locked. Rashid examined the huge padlock and noted it was locked from inside. It was then he remembered the watchman.

"We should go to Yahya the watchman," Rashid suggested.

They knew that Yahya had a built shed, as Yahya pointed out where he was sleeping that evening, in case of trouble.

When they got there, they both noticed how lifeless and dark the shed looked. There was not a single light on. They mustered their courage and knocked on the door of the shed, but there was no response. They knocked loudly several times, but there was still no response.

The next thing they did was to sound the car horn. Surely if Yahya was fast asleep, he would be awakened by the loud car horn. No matter how many times they used the car horn, there was no one opening the door.

Angry and frustrated, Rashid cursed, and started kicking and thumping the shed door. Part of him wished the door had broken down, but it was too sturdy for that to happen.

"Calm down, Rashid. Maybe he is on patrol or somewhere else."

They drove round again and found an ATV (all-terrain vehicle or quad bike) site where there was a small shed. Approaching the dark, smaller shed, they found there was no one there too.

"How come there is no one here? What are we going to do?"

In their desperation, their mind played tricks on them. They saw black ominous giants running across the beach! Sabri and Rashid stood their ground as the hairs on their back stood up.

"We are here and we are real. Everything else we see is a challenge, so let it pass," Sabri did his best to pacify his student.

They concluded they would not go back to the tent. They had to leave the beach, in case these illusions become a clear and present danger.

Real Ghost Stories of Borneo 4

Rashid called up a friend he knew would be awake and asked to be picked up. It was an emergency favor. When his friend arrived on the other side of the locked gated exit, both Sabri and Rashid left their car. They climbed over the fence and were driven back to their homes. They offered no explanation to their rescuer until the next day, when they went to pick up their tent.

They concluded that it must have been a Pontianak, even though they did not actually see her.

Sabri was not satisfied with the particulars of the incident. He suspiciously wondered if Yahya the watchman or some law enforcement agency was using a scare tactic to discourage people from camping at Tungku beach. He grew in rage at such a thought and did his best not to act on his impulses.

A few months later, Sabri revisited Tungku beach to find out if there was anything else to the event.

He met Yahya, who was hanging out with one of the ATV operators, at the ATV shed they had visited in the still of that eventful night.

"Mr. Sabri, long time no see. Is everything okay?" He could tell from Sabri's expression that Sabri was looking for answers.

Sabri told Yahya that they were 'visited' that night, but

they did not really see what it was.

The ATV operator, Hassan, keen on minding other people's business, interjected, "Ah Kedia! That Pontianak lady! Oh, she visited me once when i was camping with my brothers."

"You were camping here?" Sabri had to ask.

"Yeah, we used to. We thought it would be better to stay overnight here and not move all of our quad-bikes home. We would have to bring them back here the next day. You know, we cannot really leave our stuff here… stealing these babies can be such a temptation," Hassan laughed as he patted his rundown ATV as though it was a horse.

He went on to tell his story, which was a similar encounter at around 1 to 2 am. He described the similar laugh… yes, 'Mengilai' – a high pitched and echoing cackling that was from everywhere and nowhere.

However, the difference in their encounters was that Hassan and his brothers saw the Pontianak, a long-haired vampire in a white gown. Her hair did not fully cover her face, and yet they could not really see her face.

"That spot is her spot." Hassan pointed with his trembling finger, laughing forcibly to hide his fear.

Real Ghost Stories of Borneo 4

"You know there are 3 spots here at Tungku beach," Hassan went on.

"No. 2 spot is what they name as the laughing guy's spot. It's near the rocks." Hassan pointed to one end of the beach. He mentioned that his fishing buddies were fishing around midnight when they saw a soft yet bright light appear from within the sea. When they approached nearer to investigate, they saw the silhouette of a 'man' who was laughing constantly. His friends ran for their lives.

"No. 3 spot is the goat place." Hassan wasn't sure exactly where it was.

"Goat?" Sabri asked.

"Yes, a goat… with a human head." Hassan stayed quiet after that.

Sabri left Tungku beach and postponed any bonding program for his dojo.

The Photo

I had known 'Roy' since my 'paintball' era. Whenever I visited Kuching city, we would meet and talk about our paintball tournament days and about life in general.

Real Ghost Stories of Borneo 4

The year was 2004. Roy was in his 30s and still unmarried. He had a wonderful job, a good car, reasonable physique and respectful manners and yet he had always been unlucky in love. He was engaged a few times and somehow that went 'crash, boom and bang'.

He wanted to get married and yet, as hard as he tried, he could not find a suitable girl who really loved him. How he wished he could find his soulmate and fall in love without playing any of the pre-love games.

He always had a knack for ending up with women, whom unknown to him, were already in a relationship and were only interested in the adventures and thrills before their own marriage.

After work, he would hang out with his own posse of unlucky-in-love work colleagues, who gave each other, in hindsight, poor and misguided advice. Somewhere along the line, they were too proud to be introduced to potential partners by relatives. The modern dilemma in modern romance.

One of his close friends, Bryan, advised him to set up an online account with a popular social media platform called 'Friendster'. Yes, this was well before 'Facebook' took off. Roy was told that he could re-invent himself on Friendster and no one would really know him. No one could trace him back to his friends, relatives and work colleagues. This was very unlike Facebook. It was a chance to meet and date women and who knows, find the perfect woman.

"Whatever happens, don't tell them where you work," Bryan forewarned Roy.

"Why? I love my job as an electrician. We should be proud of being decent, honest electricians," Roy took a stand, but Bryan patted him on the shoulder.

"You don't understand women. They like to know the guy they are with is making a difference in the world, you know, like policemen, firemen, lawyers, doctors and businessmen. You choose one of those."

"I think it is best that I say I am a businessman, running an electrical company," Roy formed a plan in his head.
"Excellent idea, and you can talk about electrician stuff too. Remember our job is essential, but women like excitement and not essential."

With that, Roy set up his Friendster account whilst Bryan gave his input on choosing the right profile photo that added an air of mystery to him.

Over the next few days, Roy would check on his Friendster account. He was interested in the responses he got from the various women he contacted as well as those who added him as a friend.

Real Ghost Stories of Borneo 4

His excited work colleagues would watch over his shoulder and cheered or jeered appropriately. They were keen to give their support to Roy, perhaps so they too would have the courage to copy his strategy.

Roy eventually met in real life, a few of the women he met online, but there was no chemistry between them. Roy was getting disappointed. He was losing hope, but Bryan encouraged Roy to hold steadfast to the course.

Two weeks later, Roy found a profile of an attractive woman that seemed to share the same passion as him.

Her profile name was Mirah. Roy messaged her to meet up in person and she immediately agreed. Roy had no expectations. Her photo might not be her actual photo. His friends told him to be prepared in case she turned out to be a he! And yet he was not swayed by all the precautionary tales.

In the evening, Roy met up with Mirah, a Chinese-Kadazan, at a local secluded cafe in Kuching. It was love at first sight. The beautiful Mirah mesmerised him. She was a voluptuous woman with luscious lips and cat-like eyes. When she greeted him and smiled, Roy saw her irresistible dimples.

Roy could not believe his luck. He had found a gorgeous lady and best of all, they seemed to get along well with each other. They were almost speaking from each other's mouths. It was like she knew what to say to make him even more fascinated with her.

In the back of his mind, he wondered why Mirah was not already swept off her feet by other suitors. He could not believe his luck; he secretly thanked his lucky stars.

It turned out that Mirah, who was five years younger than Roy, was actually from the same suburb as Roy and their families knew of each other, but they decided not to let their families know. It was their way to make their relationship exciting.

Their first date went very well. Roy asked a waitress to take a photo of Roy and Mirah together. Roy noted a peculiarity after the picture was taken. There was a particular blurring in the background behind Mirah. He thought he should clean the lens of the digital camera or get a better digital camera.

Anyway, Mirah was undertaking a bachelor's degree in Accounting at the University Malaysia Sabah (UMS) in the city of Kota Kinabalu (KK). She was in her final year of studies and was on a semester break. She was returning to KK in two weeks' time.

Roy was obviously upset; he didn't like the idea of a long-distance relationship (LDR); he had a few LDRs that failed miserably.

Real Ghost Stories of Borneo 4

Yet everything about Mirah was too exciting for Roy to tuck tail and give up. Besides, she was graduating in 6 months' time. It was easy for her to persuade Roy that he could visit her in KK, stay in her apartment and promise all kinds of possibilities, to which Roy was very excited for.

And so, when the two weeks were over, their relationship blossomed from passionate friendship to the full romantic sequel.

When Mirah left for KK, Roy promised he would fly over to KK that following weekend. They kept messaging each other and when possible, Roy would call her, paying a minor fortune to listen to her sweet yet husky voice on the phone line.

He couldn't wait for the weekend. He took the first flight on a Friday afternoon, a few hours before his shift was over - which was covered by his supportive colleagues.

Roy had not been to KK since he was a child. He barely remembered the lengthy road trip with his parents. When he arrived at the KK airport in the evening, he noted how much busier it was than the Kuching city airport.

Mirah stood out from the group of airport greeters. She was waving charmingly at Roy. Knowing Roy was not accustomed to the city, she drove him for a quick tour of the city which was bustling with its city night-life.

"Let's eat, I'm starving! I must warn you. I am not like other girls; I can eat for two!" Mirah brought Roy to a popular Chinese hotspot in downtown KK.

Roy was a bit shocked at how much Mirah could eat. She had two plates of noodles.

He wondered if she was pregnant or something.

"Relax Roy, I'm not pregnant. That's just who I am. I have a good appetite and I won't get fat. Good metabolism!"

They both laughed heartily to that. Roy thought he could still be in love with her, no matter how obese she would become.

After dinner, Mirah proposed the night plan, "Two choices, you wanna go out and visit all the nightclubs or do you want to chill in my apartment and watch a movie, or whatever happens after that."

Roy was interested in spending more time with Mirah in her apartment. When they got to her apartment, it amazed him as it was a swank and spacious apartment. It was hardly what he would say a student accommodation. Unlike most students, the apartment was all to herself, and no one else.

"We could scream to our hearts' delight as much as we want to here, and none of the neighbours will hear us…" Mirah giggled, and began the ritual of disrobing, to which Roy reciprocated only too eagerly.

When things had calmed down, post-pillow event, Mirah led him to the living room, to where the television and the DVD player were.

"Shall we watch a movie? I'm a big sucker for romance movies," Mirah took lead and Roy did not object. He wanted Mirah to remain in his arms. He was already starting to count the hours he had left before his flight home. Less than 40 hours to be precise, as it was already midnight Saturday. He should enjoy the moment, but it was fast becoming a sweet and bitter moment.

Roy whipped out his phone and took a decent photo of Mirah and himself. He wanted to capture and cherish the moment. Mirah was focused on the 'The Notebook' movie playing on the TV screen whilst Roy stared at Mirah's flawless and breathtaking face, complete with symmetrical dimples.

He looked at his phone and the photo he had just taken and then gazed at her again. He thought about a happy future between the two of them. She held him tightly and uttered, "Don't worry, we will be happy together."

At first, Roy didn't realise it, and then when he looked again at the picture of themselves, Roy had inadvertently taken a photo of the mirror behind their sofa.

There was an anomaly in the digital photo. The image of the back of her head in the mirror was blurry and there were two red lights that looked like a pair of evil eyes. He said nothing, but fear overwhelmed him.

"Roy, it doesn't change how I feel for you," Mirah whispered, her eyes still focused on the movie.

"I did not say anything," Roy was nervous, these small events puzzled and confused him.

Mirah picked up the remote and switched off the TV.

"Roy, sometimes I know what you are thinking, so it is better that I be very honest with you now 'coz I am very attracted to you too and I also see a future where both of us are living and growing old together."

Roy sat up straight and tensed, "How?"

"I have a spirit that watches over me. She lives with me. It's one reason I don't have any flatmates. Sometimes they can see 'her'."

Real Ghost Stories of Borneo 4

"Mirah, are you talking about ghost spirits?"

"Yes, and no. Mia is my guardian spirit, and she can read thoughts from other people. It's good to know who have ill intentions and not."

"Oh gosh, Mirah is a nutter," Roy thought to himself.

"Roy, I am not crazy. I am telling you the truth," Mirah kisses Roy who is ever more confused, "Mia tells me you are a good man, and I know this. I want to be with you. Roy, just lay down here next to me, enjoy our moment and let's watch this movie." Mirah pulled Roy closer.

At first, Roy simply obliged. A part of him was not keen to offend his host. He reasoned he could live with a beautiful woman who was a bit crazy.

"Roy, again... I am not crazy…" Mirah kissed him on his forehead whilst still keeping her eyes on the television.

Roy fell asleep next to Mirah on the sofa. He dreamt of meeting a Pontianak with red blood eyes by the name of Mia, her face was badly scarred and bleeding and she was holding a bouquet of wilted flowers.

In his dream, he dreamt Mia was hovering in mid-air and then flying around him, screaming, "Roy, be a good boy, make her happy! Till Death, do we part!" Roy was terrified. He wanted to run away but he could not.

Roy woke up in a cold sweat. He looked around and saw Mirah fast asleep next to him. The television was still on, displaying a blue screen. It was 4am. He switched off the TV and made himself a cup of coffee. There was no way he could sleep after that. He still can't believe she rented out the posh 14th floor apartment. Her father ran a small timber company, similar to his father's. He knew his father would never sponsor good accommodation for his son.

Roy glanced out the window to watch the Kota Kinabalu night, the city now serene, orange sodium lights and the occasional neon-lights bath the empty streets. Sipping his coffee, his train of thoughts was interrupted by three black figures floating in mid-air and zooming towards the window.

The figures hit the window before he could take a step back and disappeared without a trace. He thought it was an illusion. His heart was racing, and instinctually, he sniffed his coffee, in case of an adulterant.

From behind him, a shrill voice whispered, "I am protecting her from them too." He was sure the voice was right in his left ear.

He knew he should not have, but Roy had to turn around. He saw the figure in white, that looked very much like a Pontianak, except 'she' was wearing not a white robe, but a tattered wedding gown and holding her bouquet of wilted and dried flowers.

Startled, shocked and then overwhelmed by a pungent smell of rotting carcass, Roy dropped and broke his coffee mug. He lost control of his legs and fell down to the floor.

As Roy was falling, he saw her shriveled feet were not touching the floor. Roy clambered back on his feet in desperation, ready to flee or fight the apparition, but she disappeared into thin air.

A part of him wanted to leave Mirah in her apartment, but he didn't think it was a gentleman thing to do. He packed his small backpack and sat next to Mirah until she woke up in the morning.

Mirah woke up and immediately knew there was something wrong with Roy. It looked like she knew what Roy had been thinking about.

"Roy, go on, tell me. I want to hear from you. I promise I won't laugh at you," she had a solemn face.

"Did you really tell me you have a spirit guardian with you or did I dream of that?" Roy desperately wanted to believe it was just a bad dream.

"Yes, that's what I said." Mirah nodded and bit her lower lip.

He wondered what he should do. He had heard of tales of people living with partners with guardian spirits and that never ended well. He never believed those stories. He thought they were just old wives' tales.

"You can't leave me. We have a good thing going. We can make this work."

Roy said nothing and did his best to stop thinking about whatever he was thinking. He didn't want to hurt her or make the matter any worse.

"I don't want to be broken hearted again. I want a good-hearted man to be with me. Live and love me forever."

"What about this Mia person… thing?" Roy blurted out.

"She won't hurt you. She doesn't hurt kind people. Only those who hurt me." Mirah was doing her best to maintain composure, but she couldn't catch all the tears falling down her rosy cheeks.

"I have to go. Sorry, Mirah…" Roy didn't want to say. He wondered if she could hear all her thoughts, so there was no point saying anything anymore.

He left Mirah and wandered aimlessly around Kota

Real Ghost Stories of Borneo 4

Kinabalu. He had Mirah in his thoughts all day long, but every time when the memory of her seemed so sweet, flashbacks of the hideous ghost, Mia the supposed protector ruined it.

He wondered why someone like her would have a guardian spirit. It was a curse, a prison. He concluded that was probably the reason why Mirah was still on her own. No decent man would let someone like her go. Now he knew.

Roy didn't answer the calls and text messages on his mobile phone. By late afternoon, he checked into a cheap hotel and went to sleep early.

He had left the small bedside lamp on, as he feared being alone. He downed a small bottle of whiskey from the hotel fridge and then cried himself to his sleep, feeling sorry for Mirah and his poor unlucky self.

Roy was woken up violently as he found himself thrown off the bed. Roy got on to his feet, ready to fight with his assailant. A mug, a few glasses, a notebook, his bag, and his clothes were thrown towards him at the same time. He could see her hovering in mid-air, the stench of carcass overpowering his senses.

"You hurt her! Die!" Mia grabbed his throat, her long nails dug deep into his neck. Roy struggled, gasping for his breath and started punching Mia with his right hand whilst doing his best to pry her hands from his neck.

She disappeared into thin air after a few punches. Roy called up his friends at home and asked if they had close friends who could put him up for the night.

After paying for the broken wares, Roy checked out that evening and slept on a friend of a friend's sofa. His host would stay with him and send him off to the airport the next day.

When he checked in his flight, he waved goodbye to his kind and understanding host. In the corner of his eye, he could see Mirah at the end, wearing a pair of sunnies. He had expectations but didn't expect to be heartbroken again this weekend.

When Roy came back to work, his friends insisted on knowing what had happened. They did not believe his story. Initially, they thought he was just making it up. Another friend suggested that Roy was not really into girls, to Roy's annoyance.

Roy showed the photo to his friends, but they still found it hard to believe him. The next day, he printed the actual photo to understand it better.

Some of his friends still did not believe him, concluding that the image was poor quality. The strange thing was that a few days later, both the printed photo and the digital photo in the phone itself had disappeared without any reasonable explanation.

Roy surrendered to his fate. He deleted his Friendster account and never opened any social media account, even when Facebook was the new 'all the rage'.

He deeply believed that he was destined to wander the Earth as an unmatched person, an incomplete pair. He thought about Mirah frequently, sometimes daily.

Life seemed to have no purpose, and everything from the food, the beer and whatever past-times he did was bland and meaningless. He hoped that something would end his life. Roy kept to himself and hung out less and less with his friends.

Several months later, he bumped into Mirah in Kuching city. He felt it was not accidental - pre-planned by Mirah. For the first time, he felt alive and purposeful.

After a long talk, Roy apologised for his cowardice and confessed he could not live without Mirah. They would do whatever it may take to be together. They told their parents of their relationship and their dilemma with Mia.

They were eventually married and had two children.
Roy and Mirah are now happy together.

***

"How did you manage with Mia the guardian spirit?" I asked Roy.

"She's no longer a problem."

"How is that possible?" I asked.

"We killed her."

Roy was very sparing with the details, promising me a full story the next time I visit him again in Kuching.

Real Ghost Stories of Borneo 4

The Fern Misadventure

Original story contributed by Simon.

Simon was a Biology undergraduate at the local university. He had taken an interest in studying about ferns or what was locally called 'midin'.

It fascinated him that there was little research on this primordial plant. It was a plant that had no seeds and propagated via spores, and yet it was growing everywhere in the country, surviving harsh and poor nutrient soil and being able to root itself in spots in urban settings. They could survive and reestablish themselves after a forest fire.

David, who was Simon's lecturer and supervisor, was a world specialist in ferns. This man's energy and enthusiasm fascinated Simon.

Doing research on ferns was not merely an inside-the-lab work. There was quite a bit of field work to do, which meant that Simon would have to go out into the jungle to take various measurements and conduct on-site experiments.

It is not the desire of the average person to undertake this task, as many would rather not go out into the jungle.

The Borneo jungles are hot, humid and full of creepy crawlies that are keen to give you a dreadful day.

One day, David told Simon they were heading to the Labi jungle to study the ferns in that region.

Simon was studying a particular species of fern, and his research project was on understanding the adaptations of robust ferns to various conditions found in different locations.

One would think the environment was the same in the tiny country, but some ferns can be found growing in dry shady areas with very little light, other ferns would grow partially submerged in water, whilst other ferns would grow where there was strong sunlight intensity. Simon was particularly keen to measure photosynthesis rates and chlorophyll content of the ferns.

For the trip, David's Singaporean botanist girlfriend, Cindy, was coming along. She was more into lianas, or jungle vines. She was in her thirties and her hiking attire with the long sleeves and long baggy pants could not hide how attractive she was. Like David, she was also in prime physique. She was likely a jungle trekking botanist.

"Where exactly in Labi are we heading to?"

"I text you the coordinates," David replied, and sent a

text message to Simon's mobile phone, who was literally next to him.

"4.4746236, 114.4677430," Simon looked at the strange numbers and scratched his head.

"Simon, you should know this by now. Copy the coordinates and paste it on Google Earth, duh!"

"How did you find this place?" Simon wondered how David knew more about the botanical hotspots better than most locals.

"A little bird told me this place is interesting… from a fern point of view, that is," David chuckled.

They set out predawn in David's old Japanese SUV to the location. It was surprisingly a quiet drive.

Simon woke up when they arrived at their destination. He had expected to find a signboard upon arrival, but there was none. The only sign of an entrance was a barely visible pathway into the 'Kerangas' type forest.

Simon immediately knew that this meant the jungle was dry and had an extreme condition for plants to live. The soil would have poorer nutrients, which was why the trees here were thinner and not as healthy, unlike those in a virgin tropical rainforest. By right, it was a hazard to enter this type of jungle as the branches from the trees could break any time, falling onto and injuring them.

"Be optimistic," Simon said to himself, as he watched David and Cindy enter the jungle through the pathway with no hesitation.

Everyone had their own small backpacks and hence their measuring gear. The most important thing was not to forget their water bottles. Simon was concerned about a long trek up a hilly terrain, but to his surprise it was a flat walk through the sparse jungle. Ferns grew in multitude everywhere on the bare loose ground, on small rocks, and near trees.

David suggested everyone to stay close to each other. They would look at the various ferns in their own spots but they had to remain within line of sight (LOS) of each other. The three of them were lost in their own research tasks until it was nearly noontime. Simon was keen to take his lunch break before the blazing sun would scorch him. He had eyed a good lunch break spot for the team.

Without warning, it rained, and rain heavily it did. The area had gotten very dark almost instantly. The rain was falling so hard on to them, not only had their clothes been instantly soaked, it was stinging their faces, splattering from their bodies against their glasses and eyes. Simon could not see beyond an arm's length from him. Not being able to see the others, he was all alone, and had no idea what to do.

Real Ghost Stories of Borneo 4

Simon was not sure where to seek shelter. Should he seek shelter under a nearby tree, but then risk the danger of broken branches from above? There were cases of soldiers and jungle trekkers who had died instantly when a huge tree branch had fallen on top of them.

Simon shouted out for David and Cindy, but his own voice was drowned out by the deafening roar of the torrential downpour. In the poor visibility, Simon could barely see a figure that looked like David up ahead. Simon shouted out David's name. David waved back. Simon felt so relieved, he thought he had lost everyone else. Simon sprinted through the rain. The hard ground was so much softer to the point that Simon almost stumbled down onto the very ferns he was studying.

David was not staying still, he kept moving away from Simon. The more Simon ran towards David in the rain, the further David seemed, and then suddenly David was not there. He disappeared in the grey white curtain of rain.

Annoyed, he yelled out David's name again. In the corner of his eye, he could see a person was waving at him. Simon cursed his lecturer for not waiting for him. He ran towards David, but lost him in the rain somehow.

"Wait for me, David!" Simon yelled out at the top of his

voice. This time Simon could see a silhouette of David a distance away from him. Instinctually, Simon did not immediately run to David.

Simon wondered if this was really David. Although he appeared to be the same build and height as David, he could not see his face, and more importantly, David was acting irrationally. They needed to stick together and not play games in this rainstorm.

Simon shivered in the icy rain. He was not budging; he would not run to David anymore; he would make David come to him, if it was him. Simon didn't really believe in ghosts, especially jungle ghosts, but he had heard several tales of encounters from friends and family.

He stared cautiously at the barely visible figure, waving at him, almost oblivious to the tropical downpour. When it was clear that Simon would not play chase, the figure stopped waving and stood still in the storm. Simon could feel his chest burning as it stared at him with all ill-intent.

As he did his best to wipe the ever increasing water on his eyes, Simon's heart was racing, his breathing shallow. He knew now, without a doubt, that this was not David. This was not Cindy either. He had no idea what it was, but this was no human. He was lost in this blinding storm, and he was truly alone.

Simon was struck hard on the shoulder, with such a

Real Ghost Stories of Borneo 4

force he fell down, head first onto the soft wet ground. Simon instantly turned on his back, kicking and punching his shadowy assailant, yelling out in vain for help. His assailant locked his arms and pressed hard on both his thighs, immobilizing his legs in excruciating pain.

"Calm down, Simon! Get a grip!" A familiar voice reached out to him.

Simon could make out the face of his unknown 'assailant'. It was David.

"Don't panic, you are safe! I will let you go if you don't attack me." David released him from the arm lock and then pulled him up. Simon was in complete disbelief. A part of him was unsure if this was really David.

"Simon, don't you dare run away from me again! The jungle is no place to play games!" David scolded him, to which Simon protested that he wasn't running away. Simon wanted to tell him what had happened in the rain, but he refrained.

"Where's Cindy?" David asked, to which Simon shook his head.

It was still raining badly. David paused for a thought.

"Let's get you to the jeep." David kept Simon close to

him, almost holding hands, running through the jungle to their car.

"Listen Simon, you stay inside the car. Do not leave the car. Wait for me. I am going back to find Cindy. Capisce?" Simon was too cold and too soaked to argue.

As he stayed in the SUV, he did his best to dry up any excess water from his clothes that drained ceaselessly on to the car cushion. Simon waited and waited for David to come back. The rain was not stopping; it did not die down; it refused to lessen in its intensity.

Through the rain and the heavily condensed car windows, Simon could make out 2 figures heading towards the car, but somehow the 'duo' disappeared in the rain.

"My mind must be playing tricks on me," Simon concluded. This went on for several times. Simon did his best to ignore it and waited patiently for the real David and Cindy.

It felt like forever. Hours passed and there was no sign of David or Cindy. Simon was in a dilemma. The keys were in the car. He thought he should be driving back to 'civilization' before it got dark. He asked himself if that was the moment he should have driven away and gotten help, like police rangers or even the army. He was terrified of staying overnight in the car, all alone whilst the world outside the car was running amok.

Simon prayed desperately in the lonely car. The moment he felt truly lost and hopeless, both of the front car doors flung open. The rain poured relentlessly into the car. To his relief, it was David and Cindy.

"Are you alright, Simon?"

Simon could only manage a half smile. A part of him was crying in joy.

"We are heading home before it gets too dark!" David started his SUV and cautiously drove through the rain. It was still raining, but not as badly as before.

Cindy was acting strangely. She was ecstatically rambling on and on about having discovered the most beautiful and largest tree she had even seen. She said the mysterious tree had so many species of flowers and so many vines. It was the find of a lifetime. Even though it was pouring, the miracle tree was the only thing visible in the jungle. David was such a gentleman in the way he ignored her and waited for her to calm down and rethink about what she was saying.

After they got to the main road, everyone remained silent until they arrived home. Simon and David never talked about the 'games' that were being played in the tropical rainstorm.

Dr Aammton Alias

The New Hostel

Original story contributed by Ms. Raihan

It was our first and only time hosting the Southeast Asia Games, or better known as SEA Games back in 1999. New buildings and complexes sprung up almost overnight to prepare the nation to host international athletes, support staff and more for the 9-day memorable event.

As the SEA Games came and went, there was a need to repurpose the various buildings. One complex that needed a new function was the beautiful multi-colored Ong Sum Ping apartment buildings, which was the SEA Games village. It was situated in the Capital and hence a strategic site for the various government departments and agencies vying for the site. Perhaps it was because it was so sought after that the decision to allocate the buildings took a long time.

By 2001, the decision came for one of the Ong Sum Ping apartment buildings to be converted into a school hostel for us. The SEA Games village apartment complexes were still unoccupied before then.

Back then, I was one of the student leaders in my school and as a result, I was appointed to join the inspection team. I felt privileged to be chosen to view and inspect

Real Ghost Stories of Borneo 4

the apartments.

Our delegation comprised of two teachers, a female hostel warden, our school security officer as well as five student leaders including myself.

We had gotten onto the school mini-bus and were driven to the Capital city and then to the signature Ong Sum Ping drive, a circular road with an enormous field in the middle. We tried our best to hide our excitement that one of these modern apartment buildings could be our hostel. Even our bus driver was happy for us, as he began humming a cheerful tune.

When we approached the ground floor lobby, our security officer, Anna divided us into two groups. It meant we would take less time to explore and inspect the building. Anna was an ex-military personnel. She had taken the earlier honorable discharge as she had missed the civilian life. Yet, everything about the way she acted and walked was still very much like as though she was still in the military. I wondered if she actually missed her army life.

She asked everyone to synchronise our watches and set our timer for one hour. That was the time she allocated for us to inspect all the units and then to rendezvous to the ground floor lobby.

To her, everything was like a mission. Despite this, Anna

was friendly and had an open and very supportive personality. Back then, Anna was a close friend of mine. We shared the 'suka' and 'duka' of our lives, and of course, the many jokes we cracked.

From the lobby, Anna was quick to notice the building's intercom system. She was very impressed with this. Before we all headed upstairs, she joked she could warn students when their parents were turning up.

The building was uninhabited for the past two years, and yet it was in immaculate condition. The rooms and corridors were spacious, whilst the design and general layout had been well thought of.

We visited all the units of the entire six floor building. However, as impressed as we were, it seemed eerily too quiet. To say we had the feeling we were being watched would sound like paranoia, and yet there was a subtle feeling like we were being watched.

Even though everyone had thought of the same thing, no one said a word about the sensation. In our minds, we would justify that since it had been 2 years since the SEA Games, this was the typical abandoned building atmosphere. At least that was what we tried to convince ourselves.

By 11am, both parties had returned to the ground floor lobby.

Real Ghost Stories of Borneo 4

Anna did not have to do a head count to realise that two persons were missing, which was my friend, Diyana and me.

As the group looked tired and nobody wanted to wait any longer in the building, Anna instructed everyone to get into the school minibus whilst she would search for us. The comfort of the air-conditioned minibus was too good to resist.

Anna was irate, but she reasoned that she should expect for students to be occasionally truant or even mischievous.

Anna climbed up the stairs to each floor. By the time she got to the fourth floor, the building intercom was buzzing. The girls must be playing with the intercom system.

Anna went over to the intercom, noting that the call light suggested it was coming from the sixth floor.

She pressed on the intercom call button, and spoke into the microphone, "Come on you girls, everyone else is already in the van. So, stop being so callow. When you move here, you can use the intercom every day. Trust me, you will get bored, if not annoyed with it!"

Anna was expecting to hear Diyana or me to apologise, but instead there was a deafening hissing coming from the intercom. Startled, an unwelcome thought overwhelmed Anna. She fought the thought and ignored her instincts. A surge of unreasonable anger replaced her doubts.

Anna pressed hard onto the intercom button and yelled out for the girls to head downstairs immediately or they will be left behind. Anna knew us well enough to be sure the ultimatum would scare us.

Yet, there was no response. Anna sighed and muttered under her breath, "I will give those girls a good scolding after this."

There was another intercom buzz, and then a silence. Someone on the other line was pressing on the talk/speak button and yet not saying anything. She listened intently to the silence, honing in onto the subtle sound in the silence. Anna's heart was pounding as she could hear laboured breathing, and then without warning, a loud woman's cackling broke through the silence. Anna had goosebumps all over and trembled in fear. She took several sharp and yet deep breaths and extinguished her fear.

Anna concluded this was us playing a prank on her. Since she could see from the intercom lights that the call was coming from the top floor, i.e. the sixth floor, she ran up the stairs, leaping over several steps and through the hallway of the sixth floor. She would scream in our faces, as part joke and part anger at us, for playing around with her. Anna is, or rather, was in the armed forces, and no schoolgirl could mess around with her.

When she reached to the end of the hallway, she almost kicked down the door to the main reception hall. This was where the intercom was.

Anna jumped into the reception hall and shouted, "Gotcha!"

No one was there to act surprised and laugh. The only sound there was the echo from her. There was no one there. Anna could not ignore a deep coldness in the room, but she tried her best to ignore it. She had to clear this floor, and Anna had a sense of urgency to do so quickly. She sprinted to the smaller rooms, flinging open the doors, only to find each of the rooms empty.

Where could those girls be hiding? She screamed out our names. Anna was panicking. There was one last room to inspect which was the master bedroom. This was the largest room at the end of a short corridor.

Against better judgement, she refused to approach the room cautiously. Like a military training exercise, she flung open the door and rushed into the room. There, in the corner, was a lady figure in dark clothing, her very long hair partially covering her hideous face. There was no doubt she was the very essence of evil as she started cackling.

Anna slipped on to the floor, landing hard on her buttocks. Time had slowed down to almost a standstill. She had to get out of there! She kicked hard against the smooth tiled floor, to propel herself away from the apparition.

Desperately backing away from it, and trying to get up, she was being pulled closer towards it. She turned on her front and clambered for dear life. Her legs no longer responded to her urgent need to flee. Instead, her legs surrendered and gave way. Everything faded to black as Anna felt her life force was dissipating from her body.

We had no idea the trouble we had placed Anna in. Diyana and I were tired and sought refuge in the school minibus much earlier. We were enjoying the comforts of an air-conditioned school bus.

When the rest of the entourage told us that Anna was looking for us, we waited for her for around 15 minutes. When there was no sign of her, a few of us got out of the bus and waited for Anna at the ground lobby.

We were expecting her to be there, but nothing. We waited for another five minutes, and then for another 10 minutes, but there was still no sign of Anna. We wondered what our next action plan should be. We began shouting out her name at the top of our voices.

Real Ghost Stories of Borneo 4

Soon enough, Anna climbed downstairs to the lobby. She looked disheveled, shaken, and shocked. To be precise, my first thoughts were it looked as though she had just seen a ghost. I could see she had soiled her pants. She had inadvertently urinated in her pants. I gave her a drink and asked what happened. Disorientated, we sat her down so she could catch her breath and regain composure.

After she became more orientated, she told us not to ask her any more questions. Saying no more, we helped her get back to the bus. We stayed with her at the rear of the bus. It was only once we were in the safety of our school hostel did she reveal to us the shocking incident.

We were not keen to move into the building; we preferred to remain in our old hostel. However, nothing could stop 'progress'. Our female hostel was quickly relocated to that building. To our relief, the intercom system had been disabled before our move. I do wonder who disabled it.

Dr Aammton Alias

The Jungle Mission

Sometimes, when I asked soldiers about their jungle experiences and what they had encountered, several would scoff at me. A common phrase I would hear was that in the so many years they had been in the jungle; they had not come across a single spirit of any kind.

Some blamed it on the weak mental minds of some men, whilst some would talk about 'semangat' or inner energy. If you had weak semangat, then you were more likely to see the Bunians or the invisible jungle people.

After gaining their confidence, many soldiers shared with me, their supernatural encounters. They wished the first time was their last, but it was never the last.

Private Jimmy and his men would go on regular training missions deep in the Borneo jungle. It was not uncommon for them to be in the jungle for weeks, living a life indifferent to their families back home. Such was the life of an infantryman, especially those who were considered experts in jungle warfare. They had to be like their combat daggers, always kept sharp and ready for a war that will hopefully never come.

Good commanding officers (CO) made the jungle patrols and exercises tolerable, bad leaders made such bitter experiences, whilst crazy leaders placed everyone

Real Ghost Stories of Borneo 4

in danger.

Private Jimmy and his platoon had trekked cautiously to a jungle base-camp deep in the tropical rainforest. The site chosen was next to a picturesque roaring waterfall or 'wasai', with a pool at the bottom. If it had not been for the leeches, mosquitoes and the obvious lack of modern amenities, it would have been a jungle paradise.

After unpacking and setting up tents, Jimmy and his men set out to meet their CO. They dreaded meeting up with their CO. The truth was that their CO, Roger was a bit of a nutter.

Commander (rank withheld) Roger was standing halfway on a wet cliff of the waterfall. He was bare-chested and holding his semi-automatic rifle menacingly.

"You, the new guys?" He shouted from the height as he pointed the rifle down towards them.

"Yes, Commander!" Private Jimmy shouted out, doing his best to remain cool.

Without warning, Commander Roger fired several shots as Private Jimmy and his men leaped away and ducked down for cover. To their relief, Commander Roger was shooting at the waterfall pool below. He was laughing madly and then stopped when he saw what he had unexpectantly shot.

There was a large dead turtle floating in the middle of the pool, turned upside down, exposing its pale green-yellow underbelly. The current from the splashing waterfall slowly swirled the turtle's carcass anti-clockwise.

The dead turtle was bigger than a fire-truck tire, and as it turned, it revealed its enigmatic pig-like snout. It had been a majestic and peaceful turtle, one that even the unlearned soldiers knew was a rare Borneo turtle species, now wasted by a fool with a gun.

"I caught us your dinner!" Commander Roger continued on, laughing wildly, as his laughter echoed throughout the waterfall lake.

Private Jimmy sensed this was a bad omen, and his men and he hoped that their commander will not instruct them to eat the turtle. To their relief, they were tasked to bury the shooting victim just outside the perimeter of the base-camp. Nobody wanted to attract a scavenger into the base-camp.

Lugging the carcass was itself no easy task but digging in the wet yet soft soil was another matter. Since it was an enormous animal, they had to ensure they dug deep in the ground. Scavengers such as deadly wild boars would dig deep to go after this jungle 'treasure hoard'.

Real Ghost Stories of Borneo 4

They dug with their spades until the hole was up to chest height. Then they pushed the dead turtle, which was on its shell, into the hole.

As the turtle's body fell in, its body flipped to reveal four neat bullet holes. Jimmy felt a sense of shame as he pushed wet soil and decomposing leaf matter to cover the carcass.

When the hole was filled, they packed the soil as hard as they could with their spades and boots. Then they covered the depression with a layer of small rocks. They had initially hoped to find larger rocks to deter the scavengers, but they could only find small fist-size rocks. The best they could do was to top it with broken tree branches, and then pushed more wet soil over it. Later on, they pulled larger tree branches on top of that. They were not sure if that would stop interested animals, but at least they reasoned that they had tried their best with what little they had.

That evening, Private Jimmy had difficulty sleeping. His tummy was rumbling, and he was doing his best not to have to relief himself. He wondered if it was from handling the dead turtle or from the digging. As he fought against the spasm of his bowels, he wondered if the food they cooked was contaminated. He looked at the men and saw they were sleeping soundly. He seemed to be the only one affected. What bad luck, he thought.

Private Jimmy told himself he could wait till daybreak, and he kept telling himself this for the next half an hour, until he could bear it no more. He felt his bowels could burst at any moment.

It was in the middle of the night, around 1am. He nudged a soldier next to him, a Gurkha, and told him he had to answer Mother Nature's call, to which the Gurkha soldier acknowledged and went back to sleep. Private Jimmy took a cigarette out of his cigarette pack and wedged it on to his upper right ear. He checked that he had his lighter and pocketed a small flashlight.

As he stepped out of the tent, the night was so much darker than before. The nights in the jungle were usually much darker than in the city and the villages, as the tree canopies would block out any moonlight, but never in his life, had he experienced a night as black as this.

Doing his best not to use his flashlight, he navigated by memory to the designated toilet area. Whenever he felt doubt, he used his flashlight. There was an eerie feeling he was being watched by several 'people' in the jungle. This was not an uncommon feeling that Private Jimmy had experienced during the long nights in the jungle. His only comfort from these intruding thoughts was the grave thought that he could end up soiling himself if he did not get to relief himself quickly in the designated area.

Real Ghost Stories of Borneo 4

When he arrived, he hurriedly pulled down his pants and squatted. It was during these moments he had always enjoyed a cigarette whilst relieving himself. Smoking a cigarette not only masked any offensive smells, but it also relaxed him.

Private Jimmy took out his lighter and lit his cigarette. He took a deep puff in, and without warning, a voice whispered harshly into his right ear, "NOT HERE!" It was a crisp and clear voice, followed by an angry ear-piercing scream!

Shocked, Private Jimmy dropped his cigarette and lighter and ran for his life, barely able to pull up his pants in time. Luckily for him, he did not drop his flashlight. He ran so fast that he tripped on a thick jungle vine.

Picking himself up from the ground, he assessed his situation and noted he put enough distance between him and whatever it was. He sensed he was away from any danger. However, he had soiled himself and there was only one thing he could do. He made his way to the pool by the waterfall and washed himself there. Being cautious, he muttered a prayer.

After cleaning himself up, Private Jimmy was craving for a cigarette and sighed as he remembered that he had lost his lighter and his cigarette pack was in the tent. He pondered if he should head to the tent and have a cigarette by the pool or simply have one outside the tent.

This was when his decision making was interrupted by the eerie sound of a woman singing.

The hairs on his back stood up and he felt a chill run down his spine. The singing echoed around the pool area and seemed to come from everywhere, but his instincts told him it was much nearer to him than he had hoped for. Wet and cold, he ambled away from the pool and headed towards the tent. There was no need for him to reveal his terror of the Presence that had acknowledged its presence to him.

His heart was racing, and his legs felt weak, but he could not give up there. He knew he was in danger.

"It's been weeks since you came back, Jimmy," it was a familiar voice. It sounded like his wife, but he had no doubt this was not his wife, especially not deep in the jungle, in the middle of the blackest of nights. He had to keep walking away. He picked up his pace without breaking into a full run or march.

"Keep walking, keep walking away, Jimmy. That's the only thing you know to do," The voice said, as he did his best to resist turning his head to look at it. Alarmed and bewildered, Jimmy wondered if the apparition knew of his marital issues.

"Jimmy, don't you miss me at all? You have left me all alone and unloved." Jimmy refused to turn back, and yet he could not resist it. The only way he could stop himself from all temptations was to sprint to his tent.

She was cackling continuously, her evil laughter echoed around him. Private Jimmy did not stop running even when he had reached the tent. With all the momentum he had, he jumped right into the tent. He nearly landed on one of the soldiers, who opened one eye to see who it was.

Private Jimmy did his best to maintain his composure, pretending to shiver, "That was a cold swim!"

His colleague was too sleepy to reply and went back to slumberland. Private Jimmy removed his wet clothes and changed into a dry pair of camouflage fatigues.

He tried his best to fall asleep, but he could not. Keeping awake, he thought about his wife, whom he realised he shared no more passion with. He pondered upon the future of his dying marriage. His thoughts eventually drifted to the incident with the dead turtle. He was sure the shooting of the turtle had cursed him. In his defence, he reasoned to himself, he should not be the one who was cursed as he had no part in killing the turtle. Commander Roger was the one who should pay for his 'crime'.

At dawn break, Jimmy and his men were told to take part in a training exercise. They were to set up an ambush against another team. Commander Roger was leading his team, the ambush team.

As they headed to the designated spot that Commander Roger had picked out, it began to rain, and rain heavily it did. For a tropical downpour, this was the most intense rain they had ever experienced. Jimmy wondered if this rain was real or not, as they had such poor visibility, they could not see beyond an arm's length away. The rain clouds must have blotted all sunlight as it became so dark, they wondered if they were experiencing a solar eclipse. The rain tried to drown their eyes, and splattered from all directions, even from the trees and the ground itself.

Commander Roger shouted to the men an instruction, but the deafening rain drowned out his voice. He signaled for the men to move ahead cautiously and then disappeared in the grey-white curtain of rain.

Private Jimmy asked himself where the Commander was, as they moved towards where they thought he was. There was no sign of him. The soldiers made a group decision to wait for the rain to subside than risk getting lost. They huddled together, their backs against each other, prepared to react to any danger in the dark, impossible rain. Private Jimmy could see tall shadows, like armies marching through the rain, but told no one. It must be a trick of the mind, he consoled himself as he continuously uttered a prayer chant.

Real Ghost Stories of Borneo 4

After an hour, the rain had subsided, and it was time for the men to search for their commander. They eventually met the team they were supposed to ambush in their training exercise. They too had to call off the training mission and searched for the commander.

Several hours later, they found Commander Roger nearby, face down on the ground. He had a concussion and was barely conscious. They hauled him to the base-camp and radioed for a medical evacuation helicopter to pick up their injured commander. They had concluded that a large tree branch must have fallen onto their commander, hitting a near-fatal blow to his head.

Commander Roger recovered after emergency cranial surgery to evacuate a hematoma from his brain. Even after months of neuro rehabilitation, he never resumed active duty and had to be discharged on medical grounds. His doctors could not explain the four deep bruises in his torso, which till now have not disappeared.

Dr Aammton Alias

The Noisy Neighbour

Dr. Liza, who is a specialist orthopaedic surgeon contributed the original story. She is currently working in the main hospital in the Capital.

***

One of the perks of being employed as a civil servant is the provision of free accommodation. However, it is not easy to get government housing as there has been a shortage of vacant houses.

I felt lucky that I had been allocated a terrace house, which was near the hospital where I worked. I used to live in Tutong district, which meant I had to get up very early in the morning and drive to beat the commuter's highway jam. I would usually end up in the hospital wards much earlier than the rest of my colleagues who lived much nearer than I did.

When I got the terrace house, I could wake up and leave for work at much more normal times. It also meant that during my on-calls, I could stay at home and enjoy a good night's sleep unless there was a much-dreaded phone call.

Such phone calls were usually terrible news, which meant there was a horrific road traffic accident. In case you are wondering, I get irate whenever I see selfish drivers speeding away on the motorway.

The whole neighbourhood of terrace houses were mostly occupied by other doctors from the hospital.

Even when I was on-call, I would be at home, unlike the junior doctors who had to be in the hospital. There would be many nights when I could not sleep. Perhaps it is a hospital doctor's superstition when the moment you are about to sleep, the on-call phone rings and you know there's trouble in the hospital. Hence, I cannot sleep.

During these sleepless nights, I would read up on the latest orthopaedic journals for a while and then head to the upstairs family room and perform *Tahajjud* prayers and recite the Holy Book. This was usually at around 2-3am.

I had noticed that every time I was in the family room, which was around 2am, I could hear the next door neighbour moving their furniture around.

I kept on wondering, why would they rearrange their furniture at this hour? And when would they ever be satisfied with their furniture arrangements? This kept happening on every on-call night that I had ventured into the family room.

I thought it was a test of patience, hence I did my best

to overcome the passive-aggressive person that I am - surgeons are no softies - and willed myself to be tolerable and patient.

One evening, I was cooking in the kitchen when I heard my husband calling me from the living room.

I answered him, "Yes? You called?" and he did not answer. Maybe he had not heard me, so I would peek out of the kitchen, and to my surprise there was no one there.

Strange, I thought, as I was sure it was his voice that I had heard. I looked out of the living room window and saw that his car was not in the garage. He was still at work. I convinced myself that I must have imagined it.

This also happened to my daughter, Wafa. There were a few times when Wafa would run downstairs from her bedroom believing that I had called her downstairs. Eventually, Wafa got annoyed when I told her I did no such thing. I wondered if she overheard the TV.

Things escalated after a while when our housemaid had to return home for her obligatory contractual leave, and I had to hire a part-time housemaid or amah. Judy was a pleasant, middle-aged Filipino lady with impeccable references, but every time I returned home from work, she kept reporting strange occurrences in the house.

Real Ghost Stories of Borneo 4

Judy told me that when she was drying the laundry in the backyard, she saw my husband walking towards the laundry room. She called out to my husband, but he did not reply, and he refused to look at her. He was doing his best to hide his face.

Judy went into the laundry room as she was wondering if he needed help. To her surprise, she found there was no one there. Her instincts were screaming to her that there was something sinister going on. She checked the kitchen and the living room but could not find my husband.

She looked out of the window in the living room to view the garage. His car was not there! There was no way he could have driven off without her hearing it. Additionally, there was no reason for him to be at home early when he was supposedly at work.

Every day, the part-time amah shared with me these series of unexplained incidences. Judy was spooked and tried her best to keep her end of our verbal agreement, i.e. to work until our maid returned. She did not last half-way through our agreement. It was impossible to find a replacement to fill in our domestic needs.

Regardless, my family and I did our best to ignore them. Without acknowledging what it was verbally, we all knew what it really was.

One day, I returned home to find a large mover's truck in front of my immediate neighbour's house. My neighbours were all in their car and were about to leave. I stopped them and asked why they were leaving so suddenly. The least I could do was a farewell party for them.

My neighbour, who was also a doctor, said she could not bear the thought of living in the house for another moment. She had been hearing furniture being moved from my house but did not have the neighbourly courage to tell me to stop! I convinced her it was not from my family but that I had heard the same and thought it was them.

She said she did her best to tolerate it, but the reason they had to move immediately was because one of them had seen a giant hellish black panther-like creature. Its evil red eyes shook the very core of the person who saw it, which I assumed was her husband.

That same evening, her daughter had gotten very unwell and had to be rushed to hospital. Apparently, she too had seen the demonic creature. They were too terrified and refused to stay in the house for another night.

Realising we were not the only ones experiencing these paranormal events, my family and I resolved to vacate the house immediately. Luckily for us, we were able to speed up our original plan of getting a house of our own.

On the last day of moving out of the house, I thought I saw it, if only for a glimpse. The demon, a four-legged creature that looked like a huge jungle cat stared back at me, with its soul-piercing red eyes. I didn't know if it was its way of saying farewell, but it was definitely its way of saying 'don't come back!"

I was so relieved that we did not have to stay in that damned house any longer.

Dr Aammton Alias

Don't come back @krkdile

The Dormitory: 1992

It was the year 1992. I was staying at an all girls' religious education school hostel. I had a room on the first floor of the L-shaped building.

My close friends and I were all sleeping in one corner as the bunk beds were colder there during the night.

It began after midnight, when everyone was fast asleep. My friend Gina had woken me up to accompany her to the toilet. She had a sense of urgency. The toilet was right outside of our dormitory and at the end of the corridor.

"Sur, please you have to accompany me to the toilet."

"No Gina, I'm too tired. You can go on your own, please." I closed my eyes to sleep, but Gina kept insisting, shaking me as much as she could to force me to wake up.

"Puh-lease, please, you have to. I am too scared to go. I will end up peeing here on the bed, if you don't."

"Okay, okay," I reluctantly forced my limbs to clamber out of the bunk bed, and grumpily accompanied Gina to the toilet.

On our way there, we had to stop, as a few of our seniors were actually sleeping in the middle of the room. They had their mattresses on the floor, and they were blocking the exit. I was wondering what was going on. I noticed that it was cooler here and there were a couple of dedicated fans. Perhaps that was the reason they were sleeping there.

"Gina, how are we going to get to the toilet? We can't just walk over them? Let's just go to the toilet tomorrow," I had forgotten that there was no way she could hold on till the morning.

Gina had no choice. She tiptoed and then jumped over the slumbering seniors, and to our relief, they did not wake up. Gina was getting desperate, and she did not bother to wait for me. She ran to the toilet, and it made me realise that she was actually brave enough to go on her own. She didn't need me. I was cross with myself for accompanying her.

Unwilling to walk over my sleeping seniors, I waited for Gina. I thought it would be a jinx for me to step over them.

A few minutes later, Gina came out of the toilet and again jumped across the sleeping students and headed to her own bunkbed, near the sleeping seniors.

Real Ghost Stories of Borneo 4

I had expected her to walk with me to our corner of cosy bunkbeds with our dozing friends. Instead, Gina opted to head towards her cupboard. We all had our separate cupboards across our bunkbeds, which was used to store our clothes and personal effects.

I cursed under my breath about how easy it was for her to forget about the friend that had helped her.

It was quite dark, and I could only see her shapely outline. There was a headscarf hanging on her cupboard door. Gina was fascinated by it, and she started playing with her headscarf, twisting it around her slender fingers.

"Gina, what the hell are you doing?" I was annoyed with her. I was sleepy and it looked like she was in no mood to sleep. The least she could do was help me sleep.

A voice came out from Gina's bunkbed, her body almost halfway out. It was like a groan or a yes. I was not sure.

I was asking myself, "Who is in her bed?" Before I could think of anything else, I felt quite upset and ignored that person. I scolded Gina and insisted she get to our bunkbed corner.

Gina was not listening. She was still fooling around with her scarf.

I got so mad, I shouted at her, "Gina, what are you doing

there?"

Gina said nothing. Instead, the person in the bunk bed responded for Gina, "Nothing, I am just sitting. I am going back to sleep."

It was then I realised that the person in the bunk bed was definitely Gina. I wondered about who was the 'girl' standing by Gina's cupboard and playing with the scarf.

Giving no further thoughts about it, I surrendered to my sleepiness and told Gina that we should sleep now as I was very sleepy.

The girl in the bunk bed responded with a yes and got out of her bed and walked towards me. Then we both headed to the bunkbeds in our corner. As we slowly walked towards our beds, I had a good long look at the figure in the dark, standing by Gina's cupboard and still holding on to the scarf.

It only had a humanoid shape and no noticeable human features. It remained still and hidden in the dark. Although I could not see its eyes, I sensed it was staring at me with dark intent. I should have been scared for my life. I should have screamed, but I was too tired, too lethargic to do anything else but to sleep. As soon as I snuggled into my bed, I fell into a deep slumber.

The next day when I woke up, I realised the gravity of

last night's events. I stayed quiet until it was break time. Was it a dream? I wondered to myself, but I was pretty sure I was wide awake when accompanying Gina.

Eventually, during break time, I mustered the courage to share what had transpired the night before with my roommates. Gina recalled waking up to go to the toilet in the middle of the night but did not recall noticing the thing in front of her.

Sometimes, I wondered if it was a bad dream and yet I was definitely sure that it was not. I was sure that whatever I had seen was definitely not human.

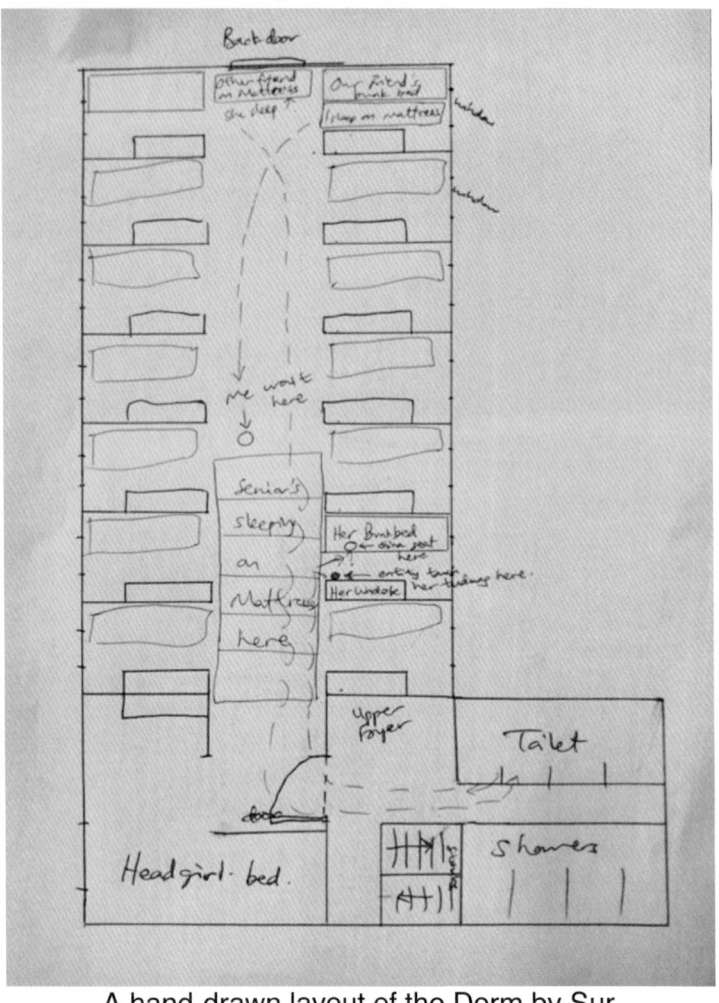

A hand-drawn layout of the Dorm by Sur

The Uneasy Student

Mamat was a Semenanjung student studying at the University. He was in his first year and one would expect him to have done his best to network and make as many friends as possible, but Mamat kept to himself.

Most people would describe him as a loner. He wore black clothing, which in other Western countries would have made people think he had a Gothic personality. He kept to himself at the University. Whenever anyone approached him, the most he would reply was with a greeting. Sometimes he would just walk away.

He stayed on the University grounds. Student accommodation halls had been arranged for him. There was a common dining room, a pantry on each floor, which he shared with the other 'flatmates'. They were not too keen with his frosty reception, but did their best to accommodate to Mamat.

They noticed something strange about Mamat. Every time he went to the kitchen where they were hanging out, the atmosphere would suddenly change. The usual jovialness between flatmates would dissipate, only to be replaced with a cold uneasiness. His flatmates did not want to discriminate against him, so they never talked about Mamat. They kept their thoughts about the difficult and frosty Mamat to themselves. No one wanted to admit that there were times where they felt something was watching over them whenever Mamat was in the building.

Time flew by, and so did the semesters. The first year had come and gone. On the last day before Mamat had to fly back home, a strange thing happened. The quiet Mamat was shouting in his room and smashing things up. Mamat was angry at someone in the room.

His flatmates knocked on his door and asked what was happening. They were concerned that someone was hurting him, even though they were pretty sure no one else had gone into Mamat's room. They were worried he was having a nervous breakdown. He seemed to fit the description well.

Mamat took his time responding. They could hear him leaning against his bedroom door, his breathing laboured, and eventually he confessed he was frustrated but he would be okay. He explained that he was in a foul mood. He wanted to be left in peace and promised not to alarm them any further.

Later on, when it was time to bid farewell, Mamat was much quieter and more reserved than before. His flatmates empathised with him but did not have the courage to reach out to him. They wondered if he would return to the university for the next year.

Real Ghost Stories of Borneo 4

Mamat flew back to his home state Terengganu, which was in West Malaysia. When he came back for the second year, he was a completely changed man.

He was still staying at the same student accommodations, with the same flatmates, who had immediately noticed the incredible changes in Mamat.

Mamat was wearing bright coloured clothes. Sometimes he sported torn denims, and his hairstyle had changed too. Some would say he was a completely different person. The dull and dark Mamat had been reborn in technicolor! They forgot the old Mamat and welcomed him into their circle of friends.

Mamat's flatmates were thrilled and often shared dinner with him. At the university, in his particular department, his lecturers too had noticed a change in him. His writing was less gloomy and much lively. Mamat was keen to ask questions and express his own opinions. He excelled in his studies, which was different to the gloomy and mediocre Mamat of last year. Even the girls in his class noticed him, and were charmed by his style, dashing looks, and intelligent mannerism. These were the same girls who looked down upon him and thought he was a despondent outcast.

After several months, Mamat's flatmates finally asked what had changed him. His face immediately looked grave, and at first, he was reluctant to share.

One of his flatmates, who was a medical student, had a stab at it, "Was it medication? Did you see a psychiatrist? You can trust us, we are good people here."

"I wish it was that simple. I don't even know where to begin," Mamat whispered ever more softly with each word, and then without warning, the lights had gone out. It was pitch black.

Everyone whipped out their mobile phones to use the flashlight function.

It turned out there was a blackout in the building. They took out the candles and lit them around their dining table.

Apparently, a nearby electric substation had a malfunction. It would be a few hours before it would get fixed.

They finished up their dinner, and somewhere along the line, their medical student flatmate asked Mamat the same question, "Mamat, what happened?"

"It's hard for me to tell you, I don't know if you would believe me."

Real Ghost Stories of Borneo 4

They told him that he could trust them, so he continued.

"Back home, my parents are worrisome parents, and they have beliefs and strong superstitions. I had two other elder brothers, but they had died when they were in university. They believe that they had been cursed, that their sons will die when they leave their home," Mamat confided as the others gasped.

"So my parents had gotten a family spirit master to protect their last son, me. This guru had assigned a warrior spirit to protect me from all harm, and those with ill intent," Mamat's gaze turned away from his friends, and there was a chilly sensation back in the flat.

"It was supposed to protect me, and yet it hurt many. Those who are gifted can see it, and they tend to flee for their lives, whilst yelling about a giant spirit, which was as tall as a house, standing behind me."

There was complete silence in the dining room.

"Even when I was walking on the streets, cats and dogs would avoid the same path as I was walking. They would scurry away and whimper in fright."

"Those were gruelling times. I was worried it would harm the people around me, my new friends, my classmates. It was overly protective. Sometimes it would talk to me, tell me things that made no sense. Did you guys ever felt its presence?"

At first, no one had said anything, but one guy in the flat said he occasionally sensed a gigantic shadow behind him, whilst another said he noticed he had always been uneasy in Mamat's presence. Everyone agreed to that.

Mamat told them that when he got back home to Terengganu, he told his parents he had enough of the spirit protection. His life was miserable, and he could not make any friends: he was all alone and he was supposed to be spending a youthful time at university. Eventually, his parents reluctantly agreed to release the spirit protector and consulted with the spirit master.

"That explains everything such as why you are free and less strained," laughed one of his friends, "You no longer have a spirit warrior ready to kick ass!"

"Actually, no. It's still here. The spirit master has retrained it and it keeps itself at a greater distance from me, unless there is imminent danger," Mamat pointed towards the field outside the dining-room windows. The lights were still out and in the darkness, they could see a towering figure, almost like a black humanoid cloud-like figure staring back at them, trying to figure out if they were Mamat's enemies or not.

The Clinic on the Hill: Part 1

I had known Dr. Alysa for some time as we were from the same high school. She was my senior by a year. It was strange that we ended up working in different clinics in the same district. She left for private practice a few years back and worked at a private clinic group that I eventually joined 9 years later.

***

Dr. Alysa doesn't remember when it first started. There were several strange things happening, but she took no notice of it, until one tragic day in February, unexplained uneasiness overwhelmed her. She could not ignore her sixth sense anymore. Their house had to be spiritually cleansed.

A close friend who was visiting had seen 'it' back in December. The Presence was at her house, sitting in their front yard, watching with hostile intentions. It was a black shadow-like figure, its shape unclear as the outlines were in continuous motion on the windless day. She knew this ethereal being was all evil.

All this time, Dr. Alysa had always thought her uneasiness was due to her imagination. When they called an 'Ustaz', who was adept at spirit containment, he could sense the presence of several spirits. Most were harmless and mere observers, but the new one that came to Dr. Alysa's house was far from harmless. It was likely to cause mischief and harm.

This explained everything. Every time Dr. Alysa came back home, the hairs on her back and her forearm would rise up and she would have a heightened awareness that someone else was there in the house, watching her every move.

The Ustaz had performed a 'ruqyah' or spiritual cleansing of her house. A ruqyah should not be confused with an exorcism: it is more of a gentle eviction.

The Ustaz suggested that this apparition had 'unintentionally' followed her home. He asked where she worked, and when she revealed the location of her clinic, he nodded and acknowledged the location as being spiritually 'busy'.

It was at that moment that everything had made sense.

Dr. Alysa worked in a rural clinic in the Tutong district. It was on top of a low-lying hill. The clinic was notoriously famous for being the clinic that was frequently visited by all kinds of jungle creatures, in particular snakes, as there was a dense jungle behind it. The firemen from the local fire department were no strangers to the clinic, as they were frequently called to remove a snake or some other wriggly creature.

Dr. Alysa had felt uncomfortable at times when she was alone in the clinic. Sometimes she could hear unexplainable sounds, like a shrill or knocking when it was really quiet. She imagined it was one of the curious or lost birds from the nearby jungle, but her instincts suggested otherwise.

She had long suspected that her clinic staff knew something else about the clinic. She had noticed that even though she wanted to finish up her backlog of referral letters and other clinic administrative paperwork, her staff would point-blank refuse for her stay back beyond the normal working hours. They would make sure that she was not the last person out.

Every time she asked why they had to be strict with her, even though she was actually their boss, they would flatly deny any suggestions of a supernatural cause. They would come up with an array of flimsy excuses, such as they were worried for her health or if she collapsed in the clinic for some unknown medical reason then there would be no one to attend to her, their much beloved family physician!

There were also times when out of the blue, she would get goosebumps all over her body. The local belief was not to say anything. One should not jinx it or 'cabul'.

At other times, she could see in the corner of her eyes, white blurring shadows zipping past. In the beginning, it terrified her, but as time went on, Dr. Alysa became curious and mustered her courage to 'challenge' the Presence.

"Who's there?" Dr. Alysa uttered out loudly one day, trembling as she did. To her relief, there was no answer. It was indeed a silly thing to do as she was sure if it had replied and reappeared before her, she could have had a heart attack, or at least faint.

Sometimes it was her patients who had supernatural encounters.

There was an elderly lady patient whose son had dropped her off outside the clinic at around 6.30am. Her son was working in a different district and had to arrive early to work. This was the only possible arrangement, if she needed to see a doctor in a government clinic. Since she was tired, she had laid down on the bench outside the clinic.

A woman calling out her name had interrupted her light sleep. When she awoke, she saw there was no one there. The voice was coming from inside the clinic. However, the clinic on the hill was not yet opened and there was no one inside the clinic. The elderly lady recited Holy Verses as she shivered in fear until the next

Real Ghost Stories of Borneo 4

waiting patient arrived.

There was also the story of Haji Ali. Haji Ali was a special patient of Dr. Alysa who was supposed to be one of the 'gifted', as he could see the Unseen spirits.

One day, the retired Haji Ali walked into Dr. Alysa's room and said out loud, "Wow, so many of them here in this room!"

It was like Haji Ali had confirmed the oddities of the day, the suspicion that she and her nurse were not alone in their room.

A chill ran down her spine. She had no choice but to stay in the room. She had to soldier on and continue seeing and treating her patients. Her nurse was heavily pregnant, so she ordered her to leave the room, have a break and then assist the reception staff. This was part of a belief that pregnant women can sometimes see the Unseen. Not willing to be alone, she asked another nurse to stay in with her.

It was indeed a strange morning as the rest of the day had very few patients in the busy clinic and it ended up being an eerily quiet day.

Dr Aammton Alias

The Clinic on the Hill: Part 2

I had known Senior Nurse (SN) Riduan for many years now. Every time I asked him for a ghost story, he had always told me of one that I flatly refuse to write up. The worst thing about the story is that I can't even tell you why I won't write it. He was always disappointed when I rejected his story. However, when I was writing up Dr. Alysa's ghost story, which involved that clinic on that hill, he shared with me his personal encounter.

There was a male nurse named Riduan who worked at the community clinic on the hill in the Tutong district. This was the same government clinic where Dr. Alysa had been working in many years ago.

One day, whilst at work, Riduan developed a pounding headache and was overwhelmed by a sudden spell of dizziness. He had not been sleeping well for the past few days due to his newly diagnosed condition, which I will not disclose.

Worried for his health, he saw the duty doctor in the clinic, whom prescribed him medication and ordered him to take the day off, i.e. sick leave. Since he felt too dizzy, he opted to sleep it off in one of the unattended treatment rooms.

The treatment room, which was the last one at the end

of the corridor, had aluminium screens installed on the windows, which ensured privacy, but it made the room very dark. Usually when the room was being used, the lights would be switched on.

Riduan had switched off the lights and slept on the trolley bed in the treatment room.

He was able to sleep for barely five minutes when he was woken up by a violent tremor. An earthquake, he thought at first and then realised there were no earthquakes in the country. Riduan thought it must have been his dizziness that was affecting his proprioceptive senses. He wondered if he had already taken his medication or not.

He recalled he had not taken the medication.. He did not want to get out of the room to get water, so he opted to go back to sleep. Not long after that, he found the bed was being shaken violently, swaying back and forth on more or less the same spot.

He woke up and yelled, "Stop it! Stop it! I am on the bed!"

He looked around in the darkness but found no one in the room but him. Riduan was not a man who would easily get frightened, and he was too unwell to move from the trolley bed. He refused to let whatever it was, rob him of his right to a much-needed respite.

"Hoi! I need to rest here. I am not well, so go away!" Riduan was half-yelling, half-begging to the empty room.

After that, Riduan was able to sleep for much longer without his bed being jostled around.

An hour later, an unidentified man had woken him up. The room was still dark, and the lights had not been switched on. In the darkness, he could see the outline of a thin elderly man wearing a 'Haj' skullcap, which was a common thing for men who have performed the Haj to wear.

He told Riduan that he wanted to rest on the trolley bed. Riduan noted that there was no nurse accompanying him. He must be one of the persistent elderly patients, who insist to have their way or the high way!

"Mister Haji, you can't just sleep here. You should wait outside with the rest of the patients. I am not feeling well, and I need to rest here please," Riduan pleaded gently to the elderly man.

Riduan tried to go back to sleep, but the elderly man refused to budge. He kept trying to push Riduan off the bed. The elderly man was not too strong and yet not weak. He was slowly pushing Riduan to the edge of the trolley bed!

"What an annoying old man!" Riduan thought to himself.

"Please Mister Haji, don't push me off, I don't want to fall off the bed. If I fall off, I may end up getting hurt!" Riduan tried to be reasonable, but the elderly man pushed harder than before and Riduan was nearly falling off the trolley. With one hand, Riduan clung on to a railing and pulled himself back to his original position.

Things quickly escalated from a point where the both of them were merely shoving each other to another point where Riduan was using all four limbs to push the man away.

"This is getting ridiculous," thought Riduan. He wondered if nurses no longer have any value in his community.

Eventually, the elderly man cursed himself and walked away. He disappeared from the treatment room without opening the exit door. This alarmed Riduan, he was already widely awakened from the minor scuffle.

"This is bull..." Riduan jumped out of the bed, his legs feeling wobbly and walked towards the light switch. He reckoned it was better to sleep with the lights on.

That was when the weirdest thing occurred. It took him ages to reach the switch, as though he was walking through jelly, each step taking such a slow time to complete. No matter how hard he tried to pick up his pace, he was moving slower and slower than before.

By the time he reached the light switch and turned on the lights, he was sweating so profusely from all the effort; his clothes were drenched. He turned back to see if the elderly man was still there, but the room was devoid of any other soul. Riduan felt an icy chill and shivered. It wasn't the cold sweat that was making him shiver.

Thinking about how troublesome it had been for him so far, he called his wife to pick him up from the clinic.

The next day, when he told his colleagues about his encounter, his colleagues looked grave and remained silent.

Eventually, they told him there used to be an elderly man or 'pakcik' with a persistent personality, who would always come into the clinic with his Haj skullcap, even though he had never performed the Haj. He had passed away in that very room, in that very trolley bed.

The Dare

Original story contributed by Hj. Alias.

It was the year 1972, when Daud, a 17-year-old adolescent boy and his posse of six friends had an argument that neither could back down from. They were not under the influence of alcohol or drugs as their village was much protected from the psychedelic revolution happening elsewhere in the world.

No one knew how the conversation had deviated so much, but Daud and his friends were trying to prove to each other that they were not afraid of ghosts. As boys who should have spent more time reading instead of fantasizing, their conversation slipped down the rabbit hole, as Daud suggested they dig up a grave in a nearby cemetery.

His friend Johari suggested they dig up a Chinese grave as he thought there were treasures and gold inside. Daud thought that was a great idea as they could prove to the other students in their school of their bravery with artifacts of gold.

There was no doubt Daud and the boys feared the thought of exhuming a Chinese grave, but they masked their fears with gestures of bravado and reinforced camaraderie, ignoring the fact of the cultural, religious and personal offense it would be to dig another person's grave.

To challenge themselves or rather to 'up the ante', so to say, they chose the next evening, which was a Thursday night. A Thursday night - considered by locals as Friday night - since the day was believed to begin with the dark night - was believed to be a 'superstitious' night when ghosts are more likely to appear!

The plan was getting ever more insane and daring. The more they talked about it, the more they felt they could not back out of the misventure, trapped in perpetual stupidity, and lured by tales of bountiful gold, the amount exponentially increasing with each mention. Daud and his posse dreamt they would be dull college students by day and by night, looters of hidden treasures in the country and the world beyond.

Daud and his posse planned their mission and packed shovels and hoes, hammers, pick-axes and chisels, kerosene lanterns, cumbersome flashlights, and not forgetting several large but tough jute sacks to carry their treasure.

At the designated time, they pedalled their bicycles to the Chinese cemetery on top of a low-lying hill. To maintain stealthiness in their clandestine mission, they slid their bicycle light dynamo off the tire thread so they could cycle on the dirt path under cover of darkness, the faint moonlight as their only lighting.

When they got to the top of the cemetery hill, they hid their bicycles in a nearby shrub and picked up their tools. The moonlight reflected upon the tiles of the graves, accentuating the cement-rock grave structures. The scene was surreal. It should have scared the living daylights out of men, but the promise of tales of bravery and gold filled these foolish boys with unfaltering courage.

They had one dilemma. With so many options, i.e. graves, they did not know how to choose which grave to dig up. The others looked at Daud to decide. Daud had not thought of a selection process.

One grave caught his eye, it was one of the largest graves at the corner of the Chinese cemetery. Displaying confidence, as he pointed towards it, the others followed him without any doubt. At least there were no obvious displays of doubt.

All the boys could sense that they were unwelcomed in the cemetery. They felt as though a thousand pair of eyes were staring at them, doing their best to force judgement on them before they commit to skulduggery.

Every step grew heavier and heavier, but Daud, their leader, encouraged them not to give in to fear. He reminded them that fear was a matter of conquering the timid mind, the trembling of his own voice unnoticed. By the time they got to their designated grave, the solidness of the structure, and the gravity of the labour needed for the task astounded them. They realised they had to break into actual stone and cement instead of simply digging up the ground.

Daud organised a rotation: two of them would use the pick-axes to break the structure, another two would use the sledgehammers, two persons would take rest and be ready to replace the tired crew, whilst one person would be on the look-out. They lit the kerosene lanterns and placed them strategically to illuminate their working area and began toiling into the night.

It was hard work to break the structure. Each loud strike made them nervous. They were worried any authorities, or the cemetery caretaker would catch them.

The boys eventually broke through the stone structure to reveal the dirt soil under it. Daud chose the most tired person to be the look-out whilst the rest started digging the much softer ground.

Johari was sweating profusely. He should have been tired but the thought of treasure got him grinning as he dug into the ground. They took breaks when needed and then began their rotation shift. It was organised work. Daud wondered if their efficiency was a sign that they were meant to be grave looters.

Eventually, the soft soil gave way to a hard surface, and a shape in the hole became clearer. It was a wooden coffin. After all that work, they had finally achieved their goal. Now they had to figure out how to open the coffin.

Initially, Daud suggested they use ropes to pull the coffin up, but no one had brought ropes. Johari suggested it was easier to break the coffin from the top.

There was no point in trying to hide their crime as the gravestone structure was already broken and cannot be mended by them. The world of the day will know this grave had been desecrated for their own glory.

Without hesitation, Daud struck the coffin hard with the pick-ax. The pick-ax became stuck to the coffin. He did his best to pull it off, but to no avail. The others tried to help him pull it off, but initially failed.

They had a second attempt and pulled the pick-ax with all their might, and when they were about to give up, the pick-ax became unstuck, flying off behind them, as the boys fell back on the ground.

Initially alarmed, and then realising that everyone was safe and nothing untoward had happened, they picked themselves up and started laughing.

Daud and Johari shone their chrome flashlights towards the coffin and saw there was a coin-sized depression in the coffin, surrounded by a ring of deep cracks. The two debated on what tool to use next whilst the others used the kerosene lanterns to illuminate the coffin.

It began with a loud crack, followed by a deafening hiss. A grey-green mist streamed out of the hole in the coffin. The mist moved on its own, forming a shape, as the boys directed their flashlights towards the mist. The outline of the mist kept changing until eventually, it formed a humanoid shape.

It consolidated and then darkened in most places. Its shape became more refined until its arms and legs could be seen and a pale face with dark gloomy eyes stared back at them.

This was no trick of the timid mind, there was no doubt this was a male vengeful apparition. The boys were frozen in place, not sure what to do.

A million thoughts flashed through their minds, as they asked themselves if they should beg for forgiveness or run for their lives.

The ghost spirit opened its mouth, its lips clinging to pieces of the other, and when it was fully opened, there was not a sound that could be heard. Daud mustered his courage and stepped forward.

Real Ghost Stories of Borneo 4

The ghost spirit let out a soul-piercing scream, and a stomach-wrenching stench overwhelmed the boys. The smell gripped the very core of the boys. They recognised it as otherworldly. It wafted straight out of hell.

The boys ran a blistering pace, stumbling and then tumbling down the dirt path, but not losing their momentum in their flight to safety. Pulling their bicycles out of the shrubs, they hurried down the cemetery hill, crashing a few times on the way down.

Johari had totaled his bicycle and had to ride pillion to Daud's.

They all holed up in Daud's room until the daybreak and spoke nothing of the incident. The grave digging incident was the talk of the village, and it did not take long for the cemetery caretaker to figure out Johari's totaled bicycle and his involvement. His 'forced' confession by his father exposed the other boys' involvement.

The boys had to help repair the grave structure with the help of their parents. They were in so much trouble, as their families felt great shame in such foolish endeavours.

For several weeks, Daud had difficulty sleeping. Every night, the same ghost spirit would haunt him in his bedroom. Each time it tried to say something to him, there was a loud shriek that only he could hear. In the daytime, he could see a glimpse of an elderly Chinese male ghoul in the mirror. Daud had to cover all the mirrors in the house.

Daud stopped hanging around with his usual friends and sought to explore his own spirituality by reading and reciting the Holy Book. His family had a spiritual cleansing ceremony done, which was also to atone for his sins. Eventually, the ghost spirit stopped its night visitations.

When things had settled down, the boys met up again, but they were sombre if not more mature in their conversations. Everyone seemed to have been visited by the same upset male Chinese ghost. In time, their neighbourhood and their village appeared to have forgotten the ordeal.

Ironically, in the 1980s, Daud married a Chinese lady whose family was probably unaware of his previous Chinese cemetery night activity.

Toyols

Part 1

Story contributed by Madam Yara.

Madam Yara had asked me to meet her as she had wanted to share her ghost story. I know Madam Yara as she is the wife of a relative of mine. I suggested that she send her story in snippets via WhatsApp messages or leave me voice note messages. I humbly explained to her I have a talent in organising information and compiling it into a story.

She refused and insisted that I meet her. She told me her story would be about 'toyols' and it made me curious about why she had to tell her story face-to-face. After much persuasion, she eventually shared her story with me over the phone. I figured the reason she preferred to do so in person: she needed me to be within an arm's length from her, in case I ridiculed her! She had known me all too well.

It all began when Yara was seven years old. One strange day during dusk or Maghrib time, she had been feeling tired and was resting on a family sofa. Everyone else in the house was busy with their chores, and she had the living room to herself. Yara put her skinny legs up on the soft sofa armrests and gazed through the windows, admiring the deep orange hues of the dusk sky.

Something had caught her eye; it was not from outside, it was from inside her house, in the very living room. It was easy to miss, and she believed they had intentionally let her see them.

On the wooden floor, she saw a group of tiny thumb-sized people staring back at her. She rubbed her eyes in disbelief; they were still there, staring and waving back at her. They seemed well-mannered and not having any ill-intentions.

She squinted harder to observe the group of tiny people who were all bald with pointy ears, like the elves in the illustrations of children's books. The dozens of males, females and even the children were all bald and had the same pointy ears. Otherwise, their faces looked like normal good-natured people.

They invited Yara to play with them. Yara would let them 'walk' over her, which was more like hiking up and climbing over a hill. The tiny people would negotiate sofa cushions like mountain climbers, walking in single files and helping each other overcome the fun obstacles that Yara had placed for them. She would try to stroke them like how one would with kittens and hamsters, but most of them did not like to be stroked.

Real Ghost Stories of Borneo 4

Yara got to know their individual names and their unique personalities. They would tell Yara stories of their adventures in Yara's language, i.e. Bahasa Melayu. However, Yara could also hear them talk with each other in their own language, which she could not comprehend. She asked them to teach her their language, but they refused, hinting it was easier to gossip about Yara if she didn't understand them.

The strange thing was that Yara thought this was all normal and considered herself lucky to have playmates. She never told her parents, her cousins or even her friends at school. Yara claimed it would be a mundane thing to do, like talking about water coming out of a water tap. It would intrigue no one.

The miniature people would come out around Maghrib time in her living room and that soon became her routine playtime.

This happened for a few years until Yara was 11 years old when they had disappeared without a trace. She would look for them, but no matter how many cushions she overturned, or furniture she moved, she could not find them. No matter how many times or how hard she cried, her tiny friends never came back. She never understood why. She did not move to a new house, and the last time they had played together, everything was very amicable, if not loving.

In time, Yara reluctantly had to accept the mysterious loss of her companions. She was convinced though that everyone else had the same experiences until one day, when she was 16 years old. She had shared her experiences with a best friend. Only then did she realised how abnormal it was.

Her best friend told her they were probably toyols. She didn't believe her friend because toyols that she had heard of or seen in horror movies were usually around 1 to 2 feet tall. The only explanation they could come up with was that perhaps the ones that Yara had met were of a different 'species' of toyols.

From time to time, Yara wondered about what she had actually seen and wondered about their whereabouts. She could barely remember their names, but she remembered their faces. She wondered if her own children would have the same experience growing up, but they did not end up meeting her much adored toyols.

However, Yara had met some people around her age, who had similar mysterious and yet adorable encounters.

Not all ghost stories are scary or horror stories. I suppose the spirits could be friendly too. Nevertheless, I am sure you and I feel the same way about ghosts… we prefer them practicing good social distancing habits.

Real Ghost Stories of Borneo 4

Part 2

Story contributed by Ahmad.

When I heard of the story of thumb-sized toyols spirits, I thought that was strange because I had only heard of the usual toyol spirit which would be around the size of a small baby. Others told me the toyol is the height of a toddler, i.e. up to 2 feet.

A friend, Ahmad, had told me he had seen toyols running around in his village, Bukit village. He described the toyols were like naked babies with pointy ears running very fast and hiding quickly.

He believed it had been the cause for several home burglaries, including one at his cousins' house. His cousin had a large TV stolen and there were no physical signs of any entry or forced entry. The only possibility was through a small hole which was large enough for a cat to enter, but not big enough for a small human to pass through.

The belief was that the small toyol would enter the house without opening doors and steal the television set. However, the question which remained was if it got in and out through the small hole, then how did it bring out the widescreen TV?

Things that went missing were usually money and

jewellery, which are small and easy things to grab, but that was the first time a widescreen TV was believed to be stolen by a toyol spirit!

Some wondered if it had a magical bag that could fit and shrink items. Of course, it sounded ever more far-fetched.

It was not the first time I had heard of toyols being used for stealing, which is reinforced when the methodology of burglars are not clear cut.

Ahmad shared a common belief that toyols were spirits captured from miscarried or aborted fetuses, and 'pelihara' or kept alive by feeding them with blood. Some say it is the blood of the owner, others say it is blood from scrupulous sources. Sometimes the toyol is fed with food, biscuits, milk or even toys! This practice is considered black magic and is forbidden in the religion. It carries tragic consequences for the toyol keeper.

Both Ahmad and I have heard of people who had been offered by their grandparents to pass down their toyol spirits. Most had declined as they have noted that even their parents have rejected the gift of a toyol spirit, even if it had been passed down from generation to generation. The ones who finally accepted their grandparents' legacy are usually those who live in the deep and rural isolated villages. The reason for their decision is still not understood.

Real Ghost Stories of Borneo 4

The Toyol burglar! @krkdile

The Cicada

The Cicada insect

In 1989, Raimi who lived in Mumong village was only 13 years old. He was a confident and adventurous boy who loved cycling around the village. When he was not cycling, he would walk around the neighbourhood, hanging out at his cousins' house and his grandparents' house. They all lived nearby, and it was a pretty safe neighbourhood. He could walk or cycle at night, without his parents worrying about safety.

Back in those days, Raimi had a freedom that could be taken for granted, which differed from the modern world of worry that we have today. No right-minded parent would let their child walk around the neighbourhood unaccompanied, be it day or nighttime.

He was considered braver than the other kids in the block i.e. his cousins, as he had no issues with riding his bicycle late at night alone. He even dared his older cousins to do so. Of course, they chickened out.

Raimi even challenged them to cycle through a cemetery which he did and had no adverse incidences. His cousins on the other hand, chickened out half-way, crashing their bicycles and leaving them in the cemetery, as they ran for their lives from an imagined army of apparitions.

Raimi would laugh them off squarely. He told everyone there was no such thing as ghosts and the only people who could see them were weak-minded people.

One evening whilst chilling out at his grandfather's house, there was a large and noisy insect called a cicada at the porch of the house. It buzzed loudly, louder than the ringing of a telephone. It was so annoying, and it kept buzzing on and off.

The cicada was an ugly-looking black insect with large transparent wings. It had rested nicely against the wooden beam of the house. Raimi found a roll of newspaper, cautiously approached it and was about to smack it when his grandfather stopped him.

He asked his grandfather why he had stopped him. His grandfather told him that the cicada insect might be from the cemetery and could be carrying a spirit. Killing the insect would anger the spirit. Raimi was respectful to his grandfather and obliged in not killing the insect.

However, when his grandfather got back into the house, Raimi shook his head in the disbelief of the elderly, tightened the roll of newspaper and challenged the cicada.

"Hey, if you really exist in there, you better come out and fight me," Raimi taunted the insect.

He smacked the cicada several times, but it did not immediately die. Raimi cursed his newspaper roll and promised he would find a bamboo stick to swat the damned cicada. Before he could find a stick, the cicada flew off with its damaged wings and buzzed annoyingly elsewhere. He laughed out loud as he realised how silly it was for him to talk to an insect.

With nothing else to do, and since it was getting late already, he started walking back home. His house was not far, but he found his usual route, a well-trodden dirt path, seemingly longer than usual. The night air had gotten cold and the bright moon that lit the path had disappeared. For the first time in his life, Raimi felt spooked. He could feel a sinister 'being' watching him. He felt paranoia grip him as he fought hard to maintain his composure.

Instinctually, he looked at one of the trees beside the path, and saw a white cloth floating mysteriously on a branch. Raimi could see a face and the outline of a figure. He panicked. He could not believe that he of all people would have a supernatural encounter.

His heart started pounding hard and his head grew heavy. He ran as fast as he could. He thought he heard someone behind him, and he looked back, but there was no one there. As he turned his head back, he saw a wall of white cloth in his path, right in front of his face. It was too close, and he was too fast to turn back.

Raimi heard a deep echoing cackle as he 'crashed' into it. The world around him spun round faster and faster and became darker and darker until there was nothing but pitch-black.

The next morning, Raimi's parents became worried about him as he had not returned home the night before. The family looked for him but it was hours before they finally found him, lying flat on the ground on the path they had searched previously! They tried to wake him up but he was not arousable.

The family had brought him home immediately. In such

usual cases these days, an unarousable person would be brought to the hospital, but his family did not believe in the miracle of modern medicine.

They had called in a spirit healer as they had seen something like this before in their lives. They knew what had happened when they saw Raimi lying flat on the ground. An evil spirit had captured Raimi's soul!

Raimi was in a coma. He could not go to school as he was bedbound, whilst family and friends surrounded his bed and recited several verses from the Holy Book on a daily basis.

The spirit healer advised the family not to despair easily as there was a lot of hard work that was needed to be done, to free Raimi from his predicament. Together, they performed a series of spirit cleansing rituals.

In the meantime, Raimi's soul was trapped in a very dark cave which had no exit. The cavernous cave had multiple floors, and Raimi was at the bottom floor. From the bottom, he could see through to the next floor up. He saw her staring down at him. She was wearing a tattered white gown, her face was partially covered by her long unkempt hair.

She said nothing to him; she did not let out a laugh or cackle. She was busy with chores upstairs and from time to time, she stared at him and that alone caused searing pain in him. Occasionally, she threw down scraps of rotten food to him, to which, being so hungry, Raimi would wolf down ravishingly. He would end up feeling unwell and vomitted out blood and pieces of meat that seemed to exist from within himself.

Raimi felt very lost and cried all the time. He was a clipped bird in a covered cage, with no hope of escape.

Raimi did not remember what happened after that. Some time later, for what seemed like a lifetime, Raimi woke up in his bed, surrounded by his family, his friends and village neighbours, who were all in 'religious attire' whilst holding prayer books.

It was a miracle for him to be alive, and to be free. Raimi was told that he had been unconscious for the past 3 weeks!

Everything changed for Raimi after that. His parents had set curfews on him, and he was not to leave the house unaccompanied. Even his grandparents insisted that he went back home early and ensured that someone would accompany him back.

He also had a lot of schoolwork to catch up, as he had been absent from school for those 3 weeks. He had neither the time nor permission to cycle around the neighbourhood. Raimi became more humble and reserved. He did not go around provoking and challenging his cousins on ghastly adventures.

Raimi told me that he remembered everything, especially his stay in that cave with that 'woman'. Even now, whether it was in nightmares or during dark lonely nights, he could see 'her' staring back at him.

FYI: As a medical doctor, I must warn you that if someone is unarousable i.e. you are not able to wake them up no matter how hard you try, you must bring them to see an Emergency doctor. I am sure the emergency and Intensive Care Unit (ICU) doctors can accommodate for any spiritual healing rituals within the confines of the hospital.

About The Author

Dr. Aammton Alias has been a family physician for almost two decades. Currently, he practices at a private community clinic.

He is the Vice-President of RELA (REading and Literacy Association). One of the many goals of this organisation is to strive for every child to own and cherish at least one book.

He is a keen conservationist and environmentalist who is deeply concerned with the state of the world the next generation will inherit.

You can reach him via:

http://www.about.me/aammton
Twitter: @Aammton
Telegram: @ElTonyX
Instagram: @aammton
Facebook Page: www.fb.me/aammtonalias

Dr Aammton Alias

What Happens After This?

Now that you have read the book, you might be wondering what happens next. You can always reach me on my Facebook page, Instagram or Telegram **especially if you have a ghost story to share** or you are simply curious on when my next book is coming out.

I have written eBooks and there is a 'universal book link' for the Real Ghost Stories of Borneo 4.

https://books2read.com/rgsob4

This way you can check which eBook platform it is currently available on.

You can also follow me at:

www.ap.aammton.com

https://books2read.com/author/aammton-alias/subscribe/23128/

or

b2rsub.aammton.com

Real Ghost Stories of Borneo 4

Upcoming Books for 2020

Bintang the Cosmocat & the Star Twins

An awesome illustrated children's' book.

This is not the actual book cover.

The Well of the Seven Kings

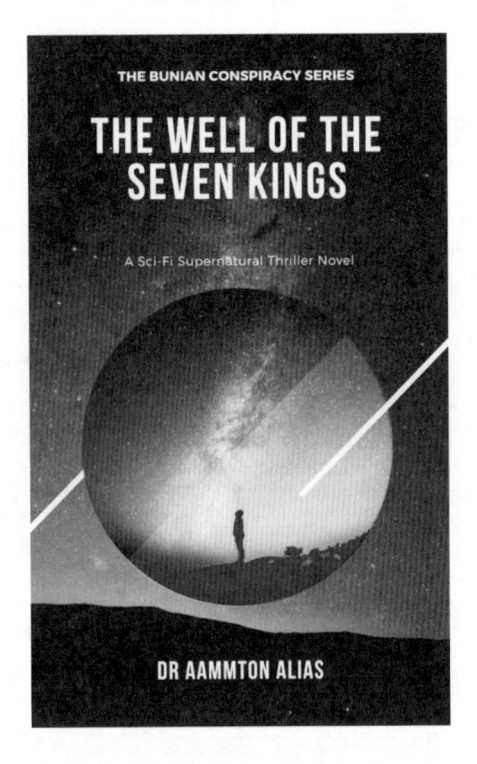

The 3rd book in The Bunian Conspiracy novel series will blow your mind away!

This is not the actual book cover.

Real Ghost Stories of Borneo 4

Real Ghost Stories of Borneo 5

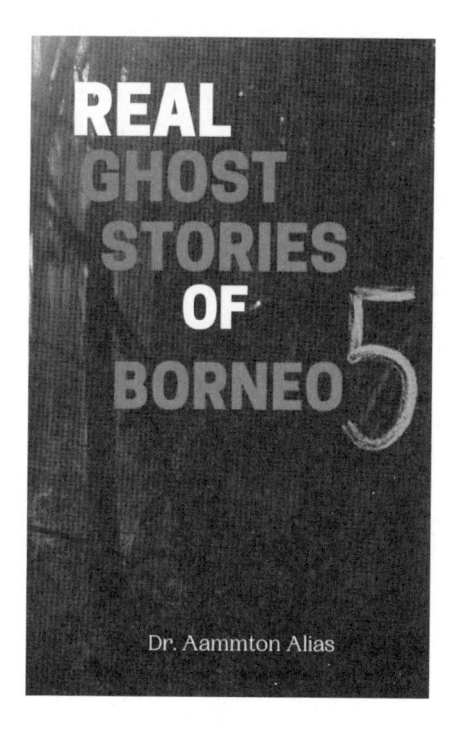

Book cover still in development

Dr Aammton Alias

My Other Books

Real Ghost Stories of Borneo 1, 2 & 3

If you enjoyed this book, then you definitely would enjoy reading Real Ghost Stories of Borneo book 1, 2 and 3.

Both books are collections of accounts of real ghost encounters, written by a family physician working in Borneo.

These supernatural tales are true accounts with a unique insight into the local population and what ails them. Be warned, very few of these stories have a 'happily ever after' ending.

Real Ghost Stories of Borneo 4

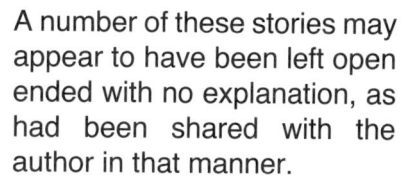

A number of these stories may appear to have been left open ended with no explanation, as had been shared with the author in that manner.

www.ghost1.b1percent.com

www.ghost2.b1percent.com

www.ghost3.b1percent.com

Please note **True Ghost Stories of Borneo** is a US Amazon version of the same book.

Killing Dreams

This is the second book in the series: The Bunian Conspiracy.

Originally inspired by the mysterious events in the jungles of Borneo island, Killing Dreams, a supernatural fantasy thriller uncovers the events in the aftermath of the horrific 3rd December Ingei jungle 'incident'.

Captain Sarin and his elite recon unit, the Prowling Tigers, are deep in Borneo's Ingei jungle tasked to investigate the gruesome massacre of the expedition team and more importantly, to find the unaccounted.

www.kill.b1percent.com

Real Ghost Stories of Borneo 4

The Last Bastion of Ingei: Imminent

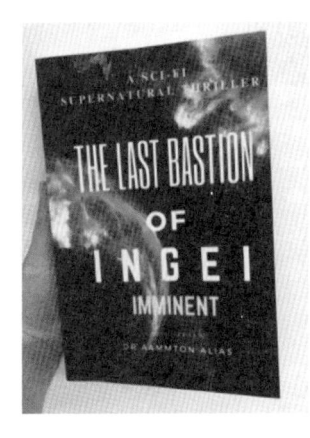

On the mysterious island of Borneo, three conservationists work together, battling against the odds. Their mission, to stop poachers from exploiting the endangered wildlife from being hunted and sold, key amongst them, the prized, enigmatic and rare 'Pangolin'. However, they are themselves being stalked by a far greater menace than they could ever imagine.

The jungle hides its secret well, but the friends are about to confront an ancient menace, far older than humanity itself, an old foe long since forgotten. Soon, the fate of Mankind will hang in the balance.

Meanwhile, a captain in the elite 5th Recon Unit is brought back to face an unspoken tragedy that no one believes happened, whilst elsewhere, recent supernatural events re-activate a secretive vanguard for human salvation: The LIMA

www.ingei.b1percent.com

Be The One Percent: Unlock Secrets to True Success, Real Wealth & Ultimate Happiness

www.book.b1percent.com

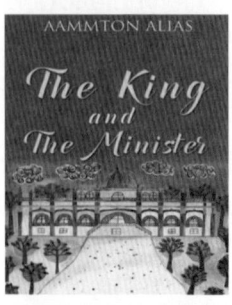

The King and The Minister

www.king.b1percent.com

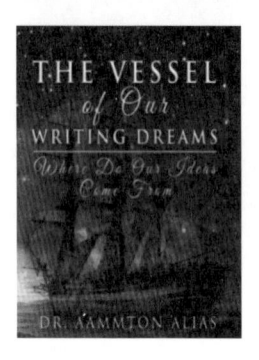

The Vessel of Our Writing Dreams: Where Do Our Ideas Come From

www.vessel.b1percent.com

Real Ghost Stories of Borneo 4

LET ME GO! How to Get Off Unwanted WhatsApp Chat Groups For Good

www.wtfrak.b1percent.com

Riki and the Dream Seed

www.riki1.b1percent.com

Dr Aammton Alias

Now Everyone Can Write & Publish A Book In 3 Days

www.write.b1percent.com

How I Became a Self-Published Author:
The Journey to 51,000 Word

Published by MPH:
www.mph1.b1percent.com